This copy of

**WORZEL GUMMIDGE
AND THE TREASURE SHIP**
*by Barbara Euphan Todd*

*belongs to*

<u>Rupert Collier</u>
<u>Tel-Cawdor 37</u>

# Worzel Gummidge and the Treasure Ship

Barbara Euphan Todd

SPARROW
BOOKS

A Sparrow Book
Published by Arrow Books Limited
17–21 Conway Street, London W1P 5HL

An imprint of the Hutchinson Publishing Group

London Melbourne Sydney
Auckland Johannesburg and agencies
throughout the world

First published by Evans Brothers 1958
Sparrow edition 1980
Reprinted 1981 (twice)

Made and printed in Great Britain
by The Anchor Press Ltd
Tiptree, Essex

ISBN 0 09 924070 X

# Contents

Dedicated to Audrey White
with thanks for her kindness

# 1 Gnomes and Toadstools

There was excitement in Scatterbrook. For months work-men had been busy turning an old barn into a house. For months, Miss Dollit had spent much of her time, skipping over mounds of wet concrete, changing her mind about the size of windows and the height of ceilings.

'I want it to look *old world*,' she said, 'but I want it to have plenty of light and air.'

For the house was hers. She was going to use part of it as an antique shop, and part of it as a tea-room. The garden at the back was to be turned into a tea-garden, and Miss Dollit and her mother were to live on the top floor.

Now, the house was finished, and it looked rather odd: this was because Miss Dollit had changed her mind so often. It was long and high and narrow, and its thatched roof was as golden as the wood-shavings in the carpenter's shop next door.

Some of the windows reminded Robin of a crazy cross-word puzzle because the glass was set in little squares bordered with lead. Another window was round, like a ship's port-hole: some of the others were quite ordinary.

Robin was feeling important because his mother, who had come with his father and baby sister to live at Finch Cottage, had been given the job of cleaning the new house. This meant that she kept the key. Usually, this hung on a dresser-shelf in the kitchen of Finch Cottage, but this morning it was in Robin's pocket because he had been sent to fetch a broom his mother had left in the room that was to be the antique shop.

He stood with his back to the Post Office wall, and Marlene Snooks sucked sweets beside him. The children were staring so hard at the house, which stood a little way back from the pavement on the opposite side of the road, that they did not hear the jangling bell of the Post Office door as it closed behind Miss Dollit. Mrs Bloomsbury-Barton was with her, and they were talking hard.

'I think I shall call it *The Noah's Ark*,' said Miss Dollit. 'Really that high narrow roof makes it look like an ark. I shall grow stiff little trees on each side of the door, and I shall sow grass in front – grass and lavender – to look like the greeny blue waves of the sea!'

'*The Noah's Ark* would be a better name for a pet shop!' objected Mrs Bloomsbury-Barton.

Miss Dollit sighed. 'Yes, I'm afraid you're right, but that port-hole window reminds me of a ship, and I AM so fond of the sea.'

'The Ark sailed on a FLOOD!' said Mrs Bloomsbury-Barton. 'Floods are horribly damp.'

'Treasure!' cried Miss Dollit suddenly. 'If I call it *The Treasure-Something* people will expect to find treasures in the antique shop.'

'*The Treasure-Something* doesn't make sense,' said Mrs Bloomsbury-Barton, who was feeling irritable, 'it doesn't mean anything.'

'I'm afraid you're right,' agreed Miss Dollit. 'Perhaps these kiddies will have an idea: kiddies sometimes DO!'

'Treasure,' thought Robin. It was almost his favourite word – a word to send his mind off on a treasure-hunt in search of buried treasure and treasure-trove and hidden treasure, and pieces-of-eight and Spanish doubloons, stored in treasure-chests, and dropped far below the sea by pirates. He glanced up at the port-hole window, wished and sighed, and spoke his wish aloud — 'Treasure Ship!'

'The very thing!' Miss Dollit clapped her hands. 'I shall call it *The Treasure Ship*, and we'll have a sign-board with a painted galleon swinging just above the door. What a clever little boy!'

'Well, I must go home now,' said Mrs Bloomsbury-Barton. 'If the house were mine, and if I were going to run a tea-shop, I should not call it anything that might suggest seasickness!'

She huddled her scarf round her neck, and stepped into the windy street.

Just then, the coal-cart drew up on the opposite side of the road, and the Rowstock brothers, who carried luggage and parcels as well as coke and coal from the station, began to carry some packing-cases round to the back of *The Treasure Ship*.

'Gnomes and toadstools!' cried Miss Dollit loudly, as though she was swearing some strange sea oath. 'Gnomes and toadstools! I must go and help.'

She hurried across the road.

'Let's go after her,' cried Marlene. 'What was that she said?'

'Dunno!' said Robin. 'We can look from the window. I've got the key.'

Inside, *The Treasure Ship* smelled of new plaster and distemper. The creosote on the beams reminded Robin of the smell of the harbour on his only visit to the seaside: they carried a tarry whiff.

Marlene rushed to one of the leaded windows, and peeped through a square of greenish glass. Robin chose another one for his peep-hole.

The Rowstock brothers had tumbled the straw from one packing-case, and had lifted out a curious object made of painted plaster. The creature had a red peaked cap, a green jerkin, and short legs with red pointed shoes.

'It's a gnome,' said Marlene. 'My Aunty Win has one on a rockery at Dimden, but its leg's broken. She keeps it by the bird-bath.'

'Why?' asked Robin.

'To look pretty. The birds don't come to the bird-bath any more. Uncle Percy keeps on saying he'll move it to the flower-bed to keep the sparrows off the crocuses. He says it's better than any scarecrow.'

'It's NOT!' said Robin, remembering the real Scatterbrook scarecrows – Worzel Gummidge and Earthy Mangold, his wife, – Mildew Turmut, the Railway Scarecrow, and Upsidaisy (the three-legged and educated one) who worked on the school allotments.

For some time, now, he had not seen Gummidge or Earthy. Winter had been turning into Spring, and scarecrows were busy at their own work in Ten Acre Field on the the downs. Since his parents had come from London, and he no longer lived with his Aunt Ruby and Uncle Tom at Station Cottage, he had not seen much of Mildew Turmut, either.

'See what they've got out of the packing-cases now!' said Marlene.

The Rowstock brothers had taken two plaster toadstools from the packing-cases, and had dumped them down beside two more gnomes – one had a leg missing. The toadstools were about twenty-four inches high. Their tops were painted red, and dotted with white spots.

'What are they for?' asked Robin.

'To look pretty,' Marlene told him. 'Aunty Win's got one, but the paint's come off.'

The Rowstock brothers were stuffing straw back into the empty packing-cases. Miss Dollit had picked up one of the gnomes, and was planting it in a little heap of wet concrete that was lying ready under one of the apple-trees. Other little hillocks of the stuff were dotted about on the grass.

A barrow full of dry sand and concrete, with a spade for mixing, stood on the path. There was a can of water beside them. It was Saturday, and the men who had been using these things would not come back until Monday morning.

'When Miss Dollit's gone, we can make a rockery,' whispered Marlene.

It was a glorious thought, but Robin shook his head because he knew that, after dinner, his mother would want to sweep out the kitchen before she caught the bus to Dimden. She would need her broom, and dinner would be punctual.

'We'll come back this afternoon,' he said.

Marlene, who had run in the opposite direction, was making a plan of her own. The great big chance of her life had come quite suddenly.

If only, thought Marlene, if only Miss Dollit would let her keep a little table in the corner of the antique shop part of *The Treasure Ship* she could sell her own things there, and make enough money to have a shop of her own. Then she would wear a black fur coat, like the woman who kept the junk shop in Dimden, and she would go to the cinema every single night.

For Marlene loved buying and selling, and collecting treasures. Every Monday morning, she lifted the lids of dustbins that waited outside cottage doors to be collected by the dustmen. Every Monday morning, she was late for school, but, always, she had found something that would come in useful one day, or that could be mended or painted, and changed for something better.

If Marlene had not been a little girl, she might have been a jackdaw. She kept her treasures in a corner of her father's loft, and she thought about them, now, as she strolled along the village street.

*There's the brass bell without a clapper – THAT would shine up. I could make a clapper from the broken teaspoon. . . . There's the vase with roses on it, and only one chip. . . . There's the plate Mrs Kibbins burned brown in her oven. . . . I'll paint that with the drop of silver paint in Mrs Bloomsbury-Barton's dustbin. . . . I'll start getting things nice this afternoon – then I'll ask Miss Dollit.*

So, when Robin returned to *The Treasure Ship*, Marlene was not there to meet him. She was up in the loft, and all her fingers were tipped with the silver of aluminium paint.

The boy heard the sound of furious whistling and, just for a moment, he wondered if the ice-cream man who visited Scatterbrook every Thursday afternoon could have driven his bicycle to the back of *The Treasure Ship*. But today was Saturday – besides, there was something different about this whistling. He hurried into the garden.

There, her tea-cup shoes imbedded in a heap of concrete, stood Mildew Turmut, the railway scarecrow. Generally, Mildew wore railway tea-cups on her feet. Her red and green flags were waving together, but they were held in one hand because she was holding something else in the other one.

As Robin came near, Mildew dropped the whistle from her mouth, and screeched, 'There's been an accident, and it's no use blaming the trains. There's been a murder – that's what there's been!'

'Coo!' said Robin excitedly, not because he was an unkind boy (his mother was fond of saying, 'He wouldn't hurt a fly!'), but because here was an extra thrill for this very special Saturday afternoon. 'Where?'

'At the station, of course!' yelled Mildew. 'Murders always happen at stations because of the trunks.'

'Why?' asked Robin, thinking of elephants.

'Because the trunks are handy,' Mildew tossed her horsehair plaits. 'Folks murders folks and chops them up and puts the bits in trunks and leaves the trunks in the Left Luggage.'

Vaguely Robin remembered reading about this sort of

murder in a Sunday newspaper.

'I know who done it, too,' added Mildew triumphantly, 'I followed 'em up by the bits of straw and the dust tracks. I got the bit that fell out when they was packing up the body!'

She stretched out her right hand, and waved the something she was holding, 'No, they couldn't get this bit in.'

The *something* was a crooked plaster leg with a pointed red-painted shoe at the end of it.

Mildew continued, 'They'd not the sense to use a trunk and the Left Luggage, so they found a packing-case and stuffed the bits in. They'll have buried 'em here. I followed the tracks.'

Again, she waved the crooked leg.

Of course, Robin knew what it was, for the one-legged gnome, its single foot held fast in concrete, stood under the apple-tree where Miss Dollit had planted it.

'That belongs to one of the gnomes,' he said.

'I don't know what his name was,' screeched Mildew, 'nor I can't remember all the Railway Bylaws off-hand, but if murder's not agin the bylaws then it ought to be.'

'There's a gnome without a leg just behind you,' said Robin.

'If the leg fits it then it's the one that's been murdered,' shrilled Mildew.

Robin pointed towards the apple-tree. 'Look! Turn round and then you'll see.'

'I can't turn round,' moaned Mildew, 'my feet's fixed!'

It was quite true. The concrete had dried round the railway scarecrow's shoes.

'Stands to reason she can't turn round. She's the wrong shape. Hedgehogs is the only sort as turns round natural.'

Worzel Gummidge, chief of all the Scatterbrook scarecrows, was speaking. He had shuffled up behind Robin, and his dear little wife, Earthy Mangold, stood beside him.

'Hedgehogs is the only things as turns *round* natural,' he repeated.

'Them and caterpillars, Worzel, love,' put in Earthy. 'Caterpillars and slaters.'

Gummidge answered sulkily, 'Things with two legs doesn't turn *round*. Hedgehogs has four, caterpillars has more.'

Earthy, who had shuffled forward, peered at the thing in Mildew's right hand.

'Beggin' your pardon,' she said gently, 'beggin' your pardon, and if it's all the same to you, Mildew's got three legs now. The third one's slipped *up*. It's growing out o' her hand.'

She stepped closer, and took the red painted foot between her twiggy fingers. Then she noticed the gnome under the apple-tree.

'Oh, Thing-love!' she moaned, 'has Mildew been rough with you?'

Her sacking cloak streamed behind her, and her blue-checked apron fluttered in the breeze as she carried the leg to its owner.

'I thought you were in Ten Acre Field,' said Robin.

He was pleased, of course he was, to see the other scarecrows, but he had wanted Mildew to finish her story.

'So we was,' agreed Worzel Gummidge, 'so we was, but we've knocked off work for the day seein' everyone else stops work on Sat'day arternoons.'

'There's been a murder, Worzel,' said Mildew Turmut chattily. 'I know who done it. It were the Rowstock brothers.'

'Murder's not work!' argued Gummidge.

'I wasn't talkin' about work.'

'Stands to reason – that's what I said. Murder's not work. It's more like a pleasant hobby to some as I knows.'

'Who?' asked Robin eagerly.

'Birds when it starts rainin', and the worms comes up. Spiders when they've set their webs in the right places. Swallers when the gnats flies high.'

'I don't call that murder,' said Robin.

'You would if you was a gnat as'd just been swallered by a swaller! Swallers dotes on murders. So'd I dote on it if ever I demeaned mesel' to start.'

Mildew Turmut was trying to jerk herself free. Her broomstick legs creaked and her ankles groaned as she tried to twist them round inside her shoes. She turned her head an inch or two, but the movement only disturbed her scarf which was a once-white towel with the letters B.R. embroidered in red.

'I've got to be back at the station in time to scare the two-thirty train from Dimden,' she moaned.

'Take your shoes off,' suggested Robin.

'Stands to reason it'd be easier to take her clothes off. Ooh aye!'

Worzel Gummidge stretched out a broomstick arm, and pointed towards his sister, who was most curiously dressed. She wore a porter's coat, whose seams were bound here and there with red piping, and a dark blue skirt. Her belt, which had been a railway carriage window strap, hung loosely round her middle. Her horsehair plaits (once the stuffing of a carriage seat) dangled on either side of her face, and she wore a hair net that was made from the mesh of a luggage rack.

'What would be the sense of that?' asked Robin, 'the sense of taking her clothes off?'

'I didn't say sense, I said it'd be easier,' argued Worzel Gummidge. 'Ooh aye! Stands to reason it'd be easier seein' as her shoes is *screwed* on.'

'The train now standing at Dimden Station will stop at Scatterbrook and Penfold.' Mildew spoke in her grandest 'railway' voice, and then her voice broke. 'I've got to scare it. If I can't scare it there, I'll scare it from here.'

She lowered her head with a ducking movement, snatched with her curious mouth at the whistle, hanging on a string round her neck, and blew fiercely.

The noise, thought Robin, must, surely, be loud enough to scare the whole village. It was too much even for Worzel Gummidge, who shambled away towards a ramshackle summer-house at the end of the path. Earthy Mangold left the gnome, and followed him, while Mildew went on whistling.

'Stop it!' shouted Robin, 'do STOP!'

With fingers in his ears, he barged against the railway scarecrow until she creaked again and again and again. Still, she went on whistling. At any moment, Miss Dollit might return to her garden. She might bring Mrs Bloomsbury-Barton with her. If that should happen, how could he explain *anything* about *anything*?

'Stop it!' he repeated.

Quite suddenly Mildew stopped, but only because her last blast on the whistle had blown it from her lips.

'Murder!' she yelled. 'Murder! Murder! Murder!'

Robin thought that the whole world must hear her. A sparrow on the roof of *The Treasure Ship* dropped its nest-building straw. A pigeon clattered its wings as it flew from the elm-tree at the foot of the orchard. Luckily, the wind was blowing away from the village so the railway scarecrow's voice was carried up to the lonely downs. Nobody heard her except Marlene, who had just come into the garden because she hoped to find a teaspoonful of concrete.

She had painted the plate with silver paint, she had burnished the brass bell, and she had discovered that the broken teaspoon was not heavy enough to make a noisy clapper. Concrete would help.

There she stood in Miss Dollit's garden, and listened to shouts of 'Murder! Murder!' and saw Robin behaving in a very queer way.

'Why are you shouting "Murder"?' asked Marlene.

'I'm not. Help me to unscrew her before Miss Dollit comes back,' gasped Robin.

Now the unscrewing might have been easy enough if Mildew had been standing on one leg only, but the children found it very difficult to unscrew both feet at the same time. Marlene gripped one ankle, and Robin grasped the other one. They pulled, they jerked, they tugged and they twisted.

After one last moan of 'Murder!' Mildew was silent. After all, she was Worzel Gummidge's sister, and sulking was in the family.

'Why was she keeping on about murder?' asked Marlene.

'She thinks,' panted Robin, desperately wiggling Mildew's left ankle, 'she thinks the Rowstock brothers murdered someone, and chopped him into bits . . . and brought the bits here . . . Hi! Where are you going?' For Marlene, shrieking loudly, was rushing out of the garden.

Something snapped. The rusty screw that had fastened Mildew's enamel-cup shoe had broken in half. Luckily it was the downhill shoe, and in another second the scarecrow's left leg was free. Robin gripped her round the waist, and twisted hard – once, twice and again.

In another second Mildew Turmut was facing the gnome whose broken leg was propped upside down against the apple-tree. Instantly, she came out of her sulk, waved her red flag, and shouted.

'That's the bit I found – the bit they couldn't get in – and that's the one that's been murdered – the one the bit fits!'

Robin whizzed her round.

'Very second class he looks,' said Mildew as she faced the gnome for the second time, and the boy paused so that he could disentangle one of the horsehair plaits that was wound round his neck. 'Second class Cheap Day Excursion. Child under twelve half price. All orange peel and biscuit crumbs, that one looks.'

Robin continued to twist as the scarecrow went on:

'Most o' the Cheap Excursion fares *needs* murderin', but it wouldn't pay the railways to let 'em be murdered, or they'd be claimin' the money back on their return tickets. Cheap Day Excursion fares is so mean.'

Robin gave a final twist, and Mildew Turmut was free.

'Mind your backs!' she shouted, as she flopped against him.

Robin saw that it would be impossible for her to walk without her shoes. He must hide her somewhere, and quickly, before Miss Dollit returned.

The summer-house would be the safest place. In another two minutes' time, he had half dragged and half carried the railway scarecrow to the end of the path.

Worzel Gummidge was standing sulkily in a corner, Earthy was watching a spider as it scurried backwards and forwards over one of her bottle-straw boots.

'Oh, Mildew, love,' she cried, as Robin dumped her sister-in-law beside her, 'oh, look at your poor feet!'

Gummidge creaked forward to look.

'Don't talk so daft!' he said. 'Stands to reason Mildew can't look at her feet when she's not got no feet!'

It was quite true. The railway scarecrow's broomstick ankles ended in knobbly stumps – knobbly because some splashes and dollops of concrete had dried on them.

She did not seem to mind, but smiled quite proudly, and said, 'Nobody'll need to tell me to keep my feet off of the carriage seats.'

Earthy made a noble offer, though green tears trickled down her brown potato face, as she spoke.

'I'll give you the lend o' one o' my bottle-straws, Mildew, love. We'll both have to hop, but we'll get along somehow.'

'I'll try to chip her shoes out of the concrete,' said Robin. 'I could do it with a pick-axe.'

Earthy was speaking again.

'I once had a lady friend as had scrubbin'-brush shoes. She took a fancy to go skatin' on the duck pond, but she weren't nimble enough so the ice froze to her bristles, and she had to wait in the middle o' the pond till it thawed.'

'Could she swim?' asked Robin.

'You need a tail for swimmin',' Earthy told him.

'Ooh aye, fish tails or duck tails or water-hen tails,' put in Worzel Gummidge.

Earthy went on with her story.

'They did say as my lady friend's hairs were rat-tails, but that weren't true. Her hairs were made out o' the string tails of pink sugar mice arter the childers had sucked the mice off o' their tails at a school treat. She'd thirty-five hairs: she should 'a' had thirty-six but one o' the childers was greedy and swallered its pink mice's tail.'

But Earthy cried a few green tears and added, 'I didn't see my lady friend again – not till they cleaned out the pond, and dragged her up to the side. She'd swelled twice the size acos she was stuffed with sawdust, and that holds water terrible. Her hairs was all green with duck-weed; they'd been white afore that. Her shoes had rotted off of her, else she'd 'a' given Mildew the lend o' them. Very kind-hearted my lady friend were.'

The word *shoes* reminded Robin that Mildew Turmut's enamel cups were imbedded in concrete. He did not mind the scare-crow being shoe-less, but he was afraid that Miss Dollit might find the shoes, and ask awkward questions.

'I'll be back in a minute,' he said, and ran down the path.

## 2 Worzel Gummidge's New Job

He did not notice Miss Dollit and Mrs Bloomsbury-Barton until it was too late to turn back.

They were both staring down at Mildew Turmut's tea-cup shoes in amazement.

'These weren't here when I left,' said Miss Dollit. 'I know they weren't, and the gnome's leg was not here either. I know it was not. I remember complaining to the Rowstock brothers that the gnome's leg was missing.'

She pointed towards the gnome.

'Look!' she said.

Mrs Bloomsbury-Barton looked, and saw Robin, and scowled at him.

There are some people who, whenever anything is missing or broken or in the wrong place, always blame the nearest child – particularly if the child happens to be a boy. Mrs Bloomsbury-Barton was one of these people.

'What do you know about this?' she asked.

Robin shuffled his feet, and did not answer.

'Did you put those horrible enamel cups into the concrete?' asked Mrs Bloomsbury-Barton.

'No,' said Robin.

'Do you know who did?'

This was a very awkward question indeed, and Robin considered his answer carefully.

'They weren't exactly *put*,' he muttered, at last, 'they were more sort of left.'

'By whom?' asked Mrs Bloomsbury-Barton.

Luckily Robin was saved from having to answer that even more awkward question because a procession of boys and one little girl, who was pushing a perambulator, straggled into the garden. Most of the boys carried sticks, and one had a camera. They seemed in no hurry to come very close. They crowded together, jostling and nudging, and peering over one another's shoulders.

'What do you want?' asked Mrs Bloomsbury-Barton.

The small girl pushed the perambulator forward, and spoke in a high voice.

'Please, we've come to see the murder!'

'Murder?' repeated Miss Dollit, who had been trying to fit the gnome's plaster leg into place, failed, and was now holding the crooked limb. 'What murder?'

The boys surged forward, and crowded round her.

'That'll be one of the bits!' said Tommy Higginsthwaite, 'look at all the blood on its foot!'

Miss Dollit gave a little shriek, and dropped the gnome's leg which fell on concrete, and broke into three pieces.

'Don't be so silly,' said the little girl, 'that's a bit from the image they put on top after they buried the body.'

The boy with the camera took a photograph of the gnome. Two other boys crawled about under the apple-tree, and one yelled joyfully when he found the footprint of a workman on the concrete.

'Come here, all of you,' cried Mrs Bloomsbury-Barton, 'come here at once, and explain why you are trampling all over Miss Dollit's garden, and behaving like hooligans.'

'I'm sure it's only a game,' said Miss Dollit. 'It must be some pretend game. They can't do much harm until the garden is set. I like kiddies to use their imagination, but I wish they'd play more prettily.'

Two or three boys had discovered the spade, and had tipped the sand and concrete out of the barrow.

'There'll be finger-prints on the spade!' shouted Tommy Higginsthwaite, 'Leave it alone!'

'Come here, all of you!' repeated Mrs Bloomsbury-Barton, and at the sound of her voice, the baby in the perambulator opened its eyes and whimpered.

'Look at the pretty gnome!' said Miss Dollit despairingly, as the whimper changed to wailing.

Just then, Mrs Marble, who worked for Mrs Bloomsbury-Barton, came into the orchard. She carried a poker, and was very much out of breath.

'Thank goodness you're safe!' she gasped. 'And you too, Miss Dollit. I came along as soon as ever I heard the news.'

'What news?' asked Mrs Bloomsbury-Barton; and Miss Dollit said, 'Do please put that poker down, Mrs Marble, you nearly broke the gnome's head.'

'I never did trust those Rowstock brothers.' Mrs Marble lowered the poker. 'Folks that will sell the coal *they* sell will stoop to anything. I never did put murder past them.'

'They said it was the Rowstock brothers,' said the little girl happily.

'Who said so?' asked Mrs Bloomsbury-Barton.

'Everyone!' answered the child.

Mrs Marble took up the tale —

'The boy that helps the milk-man on his rounds told me. You know the milk always comes late on Saturdays. "Mrs Marble," he said, "Mrs Bloomsbury-Barton's been done-in in Miss Dollit's tea-garden, done in, and chopped up by the Rowstock brothers!" I told him to tell the Police-man when he dropped his pint of milk. Then I came straight here.'

'What ridiculous nonsense,' said Mrs Bloomsbury-Barton, but her voice shook a little. 'You can see for yourself that I am perfectly well.'

Mrs Marble's voice rose to a shriek, and she pointed towards the summer-house, and to Tommy Higginsthwaite,

who was dragging Worzel Gummidge down the path.
'They've found the poor soul who was done in!'

Robin rushed along the path, stumbled over the heap of
sand and concrete, and fell flat. Other boys raced past him,
and helped to carry the scarecrow, and lay him down beside the perambulator.

Miss Dollit squealed as one of his bottle-straw boots
scraped her ankle, backed away from him, and sat down
beside her gnome. Her cheek was pressed against its face,
as the Policeman, wheeling his bicycle, walked into the
garden.

'Now, what's going on?' he asked.

Everyone except Worzel Gummidge and Robin, and the
boy with the camera, who was taking a photograph,
answered him, and everyone spoke at the same time.

Only the scarecrow was calm. He had stiffened into one
of his sulks. The slit of his mouth was closed, and so were
the slits of his eyes. Dried mud had settled in the furrows of
his cheeks, and his nose looked just like the knobble on an
ordinary turnip.

'The Rowstock brothers did someone in,' announced the
little girl, kicking at the scarecrow's hat and pushing it sideways, leaving his head bare except for the turnip-top sprouts
of hair. 'That's only an old scarecrow.'

'Anyone can see that,' agreed the Policeman.

'The Rowstock brothers did someone else in, and chopped
him up, and buried him under THAT!' She pointed to the
gnome.

'There's the spade they did it with!' yelled a small boy,
pointing in another direction.

'We've found his foot-print!' shouted the boy, who was
on hands and knees under the apple-tree.

'It was the Rowstock brothers!' repeated the little girl.

'Who told you it was?' asked the Policeman.

Of course the child did not know because, when Marlene

had rushed out of the orchard, she had met her friend Norma, and had gabbled so excitedly that Norma had not waited to ask questions but had hurried away to spread the exciting news. One boy had told another boy, the other boy had told the milk-boy, the milk-boy had told Mary, who was pushing her brother's perambulator. So the gossip had grown.

'Somebody's been having you on,' announced the Policeman, but rather gloomily because if a crime had been committed in Scatterbrook and he, Fred Wilson, could have discovered the criminal, he could have been a Sergeant in no time.

The life of a policeman in Scatterbrook was not very exciting and, so far, P.C. Wilson had caught no dangerous characters.

He glared down at Worzel Gummidge, who lay with his broomstick arms spread straight out from his shoulders, and bits of straw stuffing showing between the buttonholes of his faded shirt.

'There's no smoke without flame!' declared Mrs Marble. 'I could tell you plenty about the Rowstock brothers if I wanted to —'

'And there's also the mystery of the cups,' interrupted Miss Dollit, though Mrs Bloomsbury-Barton told her not to be so foolish.

Hopefully, the Policeman pulled his notebook from his pocket, and fumbled for his pencil.

'May as well hear what you've got to say,' he muttered.

Mrs Marble primmed up her lips. She was ready enough to gossip, but not so willing to have the gossip taken down in *writing*.

'The cups —' began Miss Dollit.

Nobody saw Gummidge's lips move, but everyone heard what he said.

'The murder was done at the station, and the bits was brought here. Ooh aye!'

'What's that?' asked the Policeman, flicking over the pages of his notebook until he found a blank page. 'Say that again.'

The younger of the Rowstock brothers sauntered up to the group. Everyone, except Mary, stood quite still. She, in an attempt to save her baby brother's life, pushed the perambulator so hard that Mrs Bloomsbury-Barton was nearly knocked down by it.

There was dead silence, and then the Rowstock brother put his hand into his pocket, pulled something out, and handed it to Miss Dollit.

'We've found this in the straw when we emptied the crate,' he said. 'It looks like a bit from one of the things we brought up from the station. We thought you'd be wanting to stick it on.'

Miss Dollit stared down at the point of red-painted plaster lying in the palm of her hand, and then she stared at the broken-legged gnome. Yes, the tip of his peaked cap was missing.

'Yes, we thought you might like it,' repeated the Rowstock brother, and smiled a kindly smile. 'What's going on – a meeting or something?'

Nobody answered him.

'I'll be getting along now,' he said, 'Bob's waiting for me. I thought you might want this – that's all.'

'Nice lad that!' said the Policeman. 'Both those brothers are nice lads – they've never given a bit of trouble yet.'

But he sighed a little, as he watched Mrs Marble and the younger Rowstock brother walking side by side out of the garden.

Two pages of his notebook were stuck together. He licked his thumb, separated the paper, and said loudly, 'So that's what all the to-doing's been about! It's the first of April. It's April Fool's Day! You've all been had!'

'Ooh aye!' agreed Worzel Gummidge, and his straw

stuffing rustled slightly. 'Stands to reason!'

'But,' argued Miss Dollit, who knew all about folk-lore as well as about country dancing, 'April Fool's Day is only April Fool's MORNING: it finishes at noon.'

'So it may do,' the Policeman peered more closely at his notebook, 'but children are children all the world over: they don't stop mischief at noon – not if they've a chance to go on with it.'

He turned to the children, and spoke loudly. 'Now be off with you! All you boys, clear off, and YOU!' He turned to Mary-with-the-perambulator, 'Don't you know you're trespassing here?'

Mary led the procession – the others, jostling and crowding like sheep that are being driven into a pen, followed her.

Robin stayed behind because he felt the danger of questioning was over, and he wanted to know what would happen to Worzel Gummidge. Miss Dollit was bending over him, and talking excitedly.

'That's Old Man Scarecrow, I know it is, that's Old Man Scarecrow, who used to stand in Farmer Braithewaite's big field.'

A faint rustling of straw stuffing showed Worzel Gummidge's disgust, and made Robin afraid that he might come out of his sulk, and say something *dreadful* to Miss Dollit, who went on chattering.

'He looks almost human, doesn't he, Mrs Bloomsbury-Barton?'

The rustling stopped instantly. Miss Dollit could not have said anything more insulting, and Robin guessed that Gummidge was trying to prove that he was not in the least human.

'I wonder if Farmer Braithewaite needs the scarecrow. I wonder if he would let me have him. That would be wonderful! I must ask him this evening.'

'My dear Phoebe,' Mrs Bloomsbury-Barton's voice was impatient, 'My dear Phoebe, why should you want a dirty old scarecrow in a tea-garden?'

Miss Dollit hesitated, as she tried to think of a reason. She was one of the people who like their possessions to be in the shapes of other things. Her favourite jam-jar was a cottage with a china roof for a lid, and a hole in the chimney through which the spoon could be pushed. Her nightdress case, though of *pink* plush, was in the shape of a kitten. Her egg cosies were chicken shaped, and she covered her telephone with a legless doll, who wore long frilly skirts.

'Well,' asked Mrs Bloomsbury-Barton, 'well, why do you want the scarecrow?'

'It would look nice and countryfied,' said Miss Dollit at last. 'After all, this *is* a country garden, isn't it? People who come from towns like to think that they are *really* in the country.'

'There's no need to make the garden look like a ploughed field!' snapped Mrs Bloomsbury-Barton, rather nastily.

'No, I'm afraid you're right.' Miss Dollit sighed, and then her face brightened. 'I know! I could use Old Man Scarecrow as a hat-stand!'

'Really, Phoebe, as a hat-stand!'

'Yes, don't you *see*? I can put him up under one of the trees. He can have his arms stretched out, just as they are now, and men can hang their hats and coats and macintoshes on him. People who come down from London always bring overcoats and macintoshes. I'll see if I can find Farmer Braithewaite now.'

But as Miss Dollit turned to go out of the garden, Marlene came back. She had heard, from Norma, the unexciting news that there *was* no Scatterbrook murder, and she had heard it at exactly the right moment, for Mrs Kibbins was spring-cleaning. Her cottage stood next door to the one where Marlene lived with her father and mother, and her back-yard was just below the loft where the little girl kept her treasures.

'I wish it was dustbin day!' grumbled Mrs Kibbins, banging a mat against the wooden fence. 'My bin's crammed with rubbish. It's a disgrace they aren't emptied more often.'

Marlene, who had just had the horrid thought that the Scatterbrook murderer might find her in the loft, and chop her into pieces, and had come down in search of grown-up company and protection, agreed with her. She, too, wished that the dust-bins could be emptied every day to make room for the next morning's treasure.

'No, I'll never get everything in. That umbrella-stand alone would take up half the room.'

Mrs Kibbins glared at a length of painted drain-pipe standing by the dustbin.

'Don't you want it?' breathed Marlene, for the drain-pipe was not even cracked, and it was painted with a pattern of bulrushes, almost as large as life.

'It takes up too much room in the passage,' Mrs Kibbins told her. 'Everyone kicks against it, and you can't sweep behind it. Take it if you like.'

Her door slammed, and as Marlene, having picked up the umbrella-stand, was staggering out of the yard, Norma wandered past.

'There wasn't a murder,' she announced. 'You've been had. It's April Fool's Day! I'm going to pick catkins. Are you coming?'

'No,' said Marlene, 'I'm busy.'

The drain-pipe was heavy, it slithered, and was awkward to carry, but Marlene did not mind. A plan – a great and glorious plan had just come into her mind. She would give Miss Dollit a present. Then Miss Dollit would like her, and might let her help in *The Treasure Ship*.

*We could be sort of partners*, thought Marlene grandly. *I could use that old washstand as a table. I could paint it up, and fix that warped tennis bat under the hole where the basin went.*

Puffing and panting, and thinking these magnificent thoughts, she staggered into the garden of *The Treasure Ship* just as Miss Dollit was coming out.

'Present for you!' gasped Marlene, letting the drain-pipe slide to the ground. 'Umbrella-stand!'

'How very kind of you,' gushed Miss Dollit, 'how very kind, and how useful it will be. Look, Mrs Bloomsbury-Barton, won't this umbrella-stand be useful?'

Mrs Bloomsbury-Barton looked at the drain-pipe in the way that she might have looked at a very dirty dishcloth, and said nothing.

'We'll keep it in the garden. Carry it over there, dear, and put it near the gnome. That's the way. It will be so useful.'

'My dear Phoebe,' Mrs Bloomsbury-Barton spoke at last, 'you don't need an umbrella stand in a tea-garden. If it's wet, people will have their tea indoors. You surely don't expect them to sit out of doors in pouring rain, and put their umbrellas into an umbrella stand!'

'But I shan't use it *as* an umbrella stand,' said Miss Dollit. She looked at Worzel Gummidge, who, still in a deep sulk, lay on the ground. 'I've another plan.'

'My dear Phoebe, you are full of plans, but I can't wait to listen to them now. I must go home and water the greenhouse.' Mrs Bloomsbury-Barton stepped over one of Worzel Gummidge's broomstick arms. 'Are you coming?'

'In a minute, but don't wait for me.'

As soon as Mrs Bloomsbury-Barton had gone, Miss Dollit turned to Marlene.

'As you have been so kind, I shall let you into my little secret. I am going to use Old Man Scarecrow as a hat-stand.' (Again there was a protesting rustle of straw.) 'The workmen are going to make an ornamental pool. When it's finished, we'll put your umbrella-stand by the water, and pop Old Man Scarecrow into it. He'll look as though he's standing knee-deep in bulrushes, and the umbrella-stand will keep his legs beautifully steady. Isn't that a lovely plan?'

Marlene thought it was, but Robin was not so sure. He did not know if Worzel Gummidge would like his bottle-straw boots to be crushed into a drain-pipe or how he would behave with other people's hats and coats.

'And now,' said Miss Dollit, 'and now, I must go and see Farmer Braithewaite. You two kiddies can pop Old Man Scarecrow into the summer-house.'

But Marlene followed her out of the garden. It was left to Robin to drag the creaking, rustling, but still sulking Worzel Gummidge along the path, and to prop him up in a corner of the summer-house.

'We did ought to be gettin' back to Ten Acre, Worzel, love,' remarked Earthy. 'Maybe the crows don't know as it's Sat'day, and they'll keep on with their eatin' work.'

'Very second class crows is,' said Mildew Turmut. 'If crows was to use the railways, the carriages'd be full o' twigs at nestin' time.'

'They'd never travel at nestin' time, and risk the addle settlin' in their eggs,' said Earthy. 'Asides, other folks in the carriages mightn't like nestlin' rooks. I'd not like to say a word about 'em, but the poor little things need comfortin' for bein' so ugly. They're all open beak with sham eyes like those men wears as balances on noisy wheels, and goes fast on Sunday arternoons.'

'Motor bikes,' said Robin. 'And the men wear motor goggles.'

'Lots o' young birds wears 'em, too,' agreed Earthy. 'You look in the next nest you see. Anyways, folks in trains mightn't take to nestlin' rooks.'

'Second-class excursions takes to anything,' argued Mildew. 'You should see their own young uns – all biscuit crumbs and orange juice and milk moustaches.'

Worzel Gummidge stirred impatiently. His arms stretched from right- to left-hand corner of the summer-house. They were spread as widely as when he was scaring rooks.

'We did ought to go back to Ten Acre, Worzel, love,' repeated Earthy.

Very slowly Gummidge opened his eyes, and very slowly his lips moved.

'I'm not goin' back to Ten Acre, seein' I've a new job.'

'Worzel, LOVE!' Earthy's voice sounded very excited. 'What sort o' new job?'

'I'm a hat-stand!' said Gummidge proudly, 'Ooh aye!'

'You aren't standin' on no hats, Worzel, not as I can see. Beggin' your pardon, and if it's all the same to you, you aren't standin' on no hats.'

Earthy peered downwards. 'Leastways if you are standin' on hats, they casn't be no bigger than'd fit insecks.'

'Stands to reason I'm not standin' on hats seein' as there aren't no hats to stand on. The hats'll come later.'

Earthy peered out of the summer-house, as though she expected to see a procession of hats bowling along towards her husband. She asked in a puzzled voice, 'Does it feel grand bein' a hat-stand?'

'IF I knowed how a hat-stand feels I'd know if it feels nice bein' a hat-stand. Ooh aye! I've not had the chance o' meetin' any other hat-stands yet. Nobody knows what they feels like till they've talked their feelin's over. Differ things has differ feelin's. Things the shape o' humans don't like havin' pins stuck in 'em – I've heard human babies objectin'. Things the shape o' hedgehogs don't worry.'

'I hopes they doesn't,' said Earthy. 'It don't abear thinkin' of to think as their bristles goes through, and pricks their poor little innards all day and all night.' A few green tears rolled down her cheeks. 'It's pitiful to look like a scrubbin' brush let alone actin' like a scrubbin' brush to your own tender innards, day in day out, winter and summer.'

'Hedgehogs rests all winter,' Gummidge told her.

'That only gives the bristles the chanst to grow longer, and scrub the tender innards harder at spring-cleanin' time.'

Mildew Turmut interrupted, 'I've got to get back to the railway allotment. Give me a lend o' your boots, Worzel. You'll not need 'em, seein' as you're a hat-stand.'

'Stands to reason I'll not give you a lend o' my bottle-straws – not till I've had a chat with some more hat-stands and found out if they wears boots.'

'They don't!' said Robin. 'There's a hat-stand in Mrs Bloomsbury-Barton's hall.'

'Maybe I'll go along and have a chat with it this evenin'. Anyways I'll not give Mildew the lend o' my boots. Centipedes gets on without 'em.'

'Centipedes has more feet to balance with,' replied Mildew sulkily, 'and their legs is shorter.'

Gummidge scowled at her. 'I'd not demean mesel' to stare at centipedes' legs. No more would centipedes demean 'emsel's to borrow boots off of other centipedes if other centipedes wore boots. Stands to reason.'

Earthy, kindly as ever, stretched out her twiggy fingers, and stroked Mildew Turmut's red flag.

'I'd give you a lend o' my boots, Mildew, love. I'd give you a lend o' them willin', but seein' I've got to be a hat-stand I may need 'em for the job.'

'You're not a hat-stand!' Worzel Gummidge spoke quite furiously to his gentle wife. 'You're not a hat-stand, and you'll never be a hat-stand neither.'

'Oh, Worzel, love!' Earthy wrung her hands until her fingers made tiny crackling sounds, like the whisper of hedges when drowsy birds stir in the branches. 'Why won't I be a hat-stand?'

'Acos,' said Gummidge grandly, 'acos you've not had no invite. I were ASKED by Miss Dollit.'

'But husbins and wives allus does the same things together!'

'Don't talk so daft. Hen wives sit on eggs while the husbins keep on crowin'. Spider wives EATS their husbins!'

Green tears flowed down Earthy Mangold's cheeks, and she murmured, 'I never would!'

Worzel Gummidge continued, 'Blackbird husbins wears shiny black, and has bright yeller beaks, and the wives is mottled. Human husbins stays out o' the way acos the wives makes the houses too clean for 'em.'

Mildew Turmut interrupted, 'Human travellin' husbins goes in smokin' carriages so's to keep away from the wives and babies.'

'Ooh aye!' agreed Gummidge. 'Stands to reason husbins and wives does differ things. I'll not be married to a hat-stand! You'd best find a job for yoursel', Earthy. Go and be a luggage rack on the railways if you wants to.'

'She's the wrong shape for that,' said Mildew Turmut. 'She'd need stretching out till holes came in her. Luggage racks has lots o' holes, so's the water from the flowers folks takes to Lunnon can trickle through. Give me a lend o' your boots, Earthy.'

But Earthy, sobbing a little because she could not be a hat-stand, was half hopping and half shuffling out of the summer-house. Her sacking cloak trailed behind her, as she made her way towards the orchard at the end of the garden.

Perhaps Worzel Gummidge's queer conscience troubled him a little, for he murmured, 'I don't know as there *is* she-hat-stands!'

Then he stretched out his arms again, stiffened his legs, closed his eyes, and said, 'Leave me be to practise my new job.'

Robin left him and went home to supper.

# 3 Worzel Gummidge Pays a Call

Miss Dollit was very happy indeed. Farmer Braithewaite had agreed that she might borrow Worzel Gummidge so that she could set him up as a hat-stand in her tea-garden.

That was not the only reason for her happiness. During her visit to the farm she had met a pet lamb, and the little creature had taken a fancy to her. It jumped about on its ridiculous stubby legs, it rubbed its soft nose against her, and bleated sadly.

'Animals always know who like them,' said Miss Dollit, 'they know the people they can trust.'

'That's a fact!' said Mrs Braithewaite, and she winked at her husband.

The truth was that the lamb was becoming rather a nuisance. It was, as Mrs Braithewaite said so often, 'into everything'. It skipped into muddy puddles as it followed her across the farm-yard. Then, without troubling even to shake its woolly gaiters, it would skip into a bowl of cream, and prance until the cream turned from golden to grey.

'If only it were mine!' breathed Miss Dollit.

Again Mrs Braithewaite winked at her husband.

'I'm sure we'd be glad to let you have it,' she said. 'It needs more time than we can give it, but it would make a perfect pet for a single lady.'

Miss Dollit clutched the lamb, as though she were afraid that Mrs Braithewaite would change her mind.

'We could send up a drop of extra milk twice a day,'

added Farmer Braithewaite. 'We've brought it up on the bottle ever since its mother died. It has milk twice a day but it's beginning to fancy grass now – grass and greenstuff.' He scowled as he remembered the row of seedling lettuces which the lamb had fancied during one of its trips round the kitchen garden.

'It can *gambol* on Mrs Bloomsbury-Barton's lawn!' declared Miss Dollit, 'and when I move into my *Treasure Ship* it can live in the orchard there. I shall grow mustard and cress for it. No, perhaps mustard would be too strong. Do you think it would like cress?'

Mrs Braithewaite knew that the lamb liked cress. She had planned to have mustard and cress sandwiches for a treat on Sunday, but the lamb had enjoyed the 'treat' as a mid-morning snack.

'I shall take the greatest care of the dear little thing,' said Miss Dollit, as she left the farm.

Mrs Bloomsbury-Barton was not very pleased to see the lamb or its bottle, and Mrs Marble was very displeased when Miss Dollit put it down in the hall.

'It's not going to live in the house, surely?' she said as the lamb danced about on the parquet-flooring, and waggled its long tail as though to show it expected supper. 'Look at it now, breathing against the meogany hat-stand that I polished only this morning.'

'Of course it is not going to live in the house,' said Mrs Bloomsbury-Barton decidedly. 'It can sleep in the wood-wood-shed until Miss Dollit leaves here. In the daytime it can be tethered on the lawn: it cannot do much harm there.'

Mrs Marble sniffed doubtfully, as the lamb rubbed its soft and dewy nose against the hat-stand, and left little smears of moisture on the polished wood.

'I think it slept in the kitchen at the farm,' said Miss Dollit hopefully. 'We don't want the poor little thing to be lonely, do we?'

'It'll be lonely if it sets foot in my kitchen.' Mrs Marble flicked at the lamb with the corner of her apron, and began to polish the hat-stand again. 'The instant that creature comes into my kitchen out I go.'

The lamb bleated, and skipped towards Miss Dollit, while Mrs Marble rubbed the hat-stand violently. It was an ugly piece of furniture. Large curving wooden hooks sprouted from it in all directions. It stood on cross-bars, and had four carved feet.

At the moment, it looked like an over-dressed and very, very respectable elderly lady scarecrow because a garden hat of Mrs Bloomsbury-Barton's perched on the top of it. Below the hat was a small oval mirror, and below the mirror hung Miss Dollit's tweed cloak. Hooks on either side held a woollen scarf and a chiffon stole.

'I've worn me fingers to the bone polishing this meogany,' said Mrs Marble savagely, 'but it's not to be expected I should wear the bones down to the joints polishing away lamb's nose-marks!'

'Take it to the woodshed, Phoebe, *do*,' begged Mrs Bloomsbury-Barton, 'it can have its supper there.'

It so happened that directly after Mrs Bloomsbury-Barton and Miss Dollit had had their suppers, and after Mrs Marble had washed up and gone home, and after the lamb, with much tail-wagging, had enjoyed a bottle of warm milk, the electricity failed. When candles had been lit in the drawing-room and the hall, and Mrs Bloomsbury-Barton had settled down to knit, Miss Dollit lighted a hurricane lantern, and went to visit her lamb.

Mrs Bloomsbury-Barton, trying to read her knitting-pattern by candle-light, did not hear the sound of her front door being pushed open, or the sheep-like cough of the scarecrow.

Worzel Gummidge was the visitor. He had come to have his chat with the hat-stand.

'Evenin'!' he said.

Naturally, the hat-stand made no reply.

'Evenin',' repeated Gummidge. 'I've come to find out how *our* sort goes on.'

The wind, blowing in through the half open door, stirred the chiffon scarf on the hat-stand.

'It's no use shakin' your rags at me!' said Gummidge, 'I'm not a crow: I'm a hat-stand, same as you. It's only acos I'm new to the job that I wants to know how to go on. If you was to come to Ten Acre to be learned how to scare crows, I'd learn you if you asked me civil.'

There was a candle on the oak chest that stood against the opposite wall. The wick flared and wavered in the breeze so that it threw strange shadows on to the oval mirror between Mrs Bloomsbury-Barton's hat and Miss Dollit's cloak.

Worzel Gummidge leaned forward until he saw his own face reflected wildly in the mirror. 'Anyone can see as we're relations,' he muttered. 'You've a turnip face same as me. Ooh aye, but I'd not demean mesel' to wear a hat like that. Stands to reason I'd not.'

The hat, which was straw-coloured, was trimmed with artificial roses and a swathe of black veiling.

The flickering light of the candle made the reflected face look as though it were smiling.

'Don't stand grinnin' at me!' shouted Gummidge.

A scowl appeared on the face of the mirror.

'Have you got bottle-straw boots?' asked Gummidge.

He creaked forward. His joints cracked, as slowly, very slowly, he managed to bend himself almost double.

'You've four feet,' he muttered, 'you've animile's feet. I'd sooner stay standin' than have animile feet.'

It was quite true. The hat-stand's cross-bars were perched on carved lion-claws.

Gummidge straightened himself, and asked, 'How do

you go on when all four feet wants to walk in differ ways?'

There was no answer from the hat-stand. It stood there provokingly, so provokingly that the scarecrow kicked it with the scratchy toe of his bottle-straw boot.

Mrs Bloomsbury-Barton saw him. She had left the drawing-room because she needed another candle. The light in the hall was so dim that she only saw an unrecognizable figure.

She gave a little scream, and then asked bravely, 'Who are you, and what do you want?'

'I come up for a chat,' replied Worzel Gummidge, shuffling backwards so that his shabby coat sleeve knocked against the candle.

In another second the hall was in darkness except for a shaft of moonlight, streaming in through the open door.

'Who are you?' repeated Mrs Bloomsbury-Barton. 'Why didn't you ring the bell or knock the knocker?'

'Don't talk so daft!'

The scarecrow's answer made Mrs Bloomsbury-Barton quite sure that he was a burglar. It would have been daft (though she would never have used such a word) for a burglar to knock or to ring.

'Don't talk so daft! Stands to reason I come for a chat wi' one o' my relations.'

Mrs Bloomsbury-Barton decided that if her visitor was not a burglar, he must be a lunatic. Somewhere she had read that it is dangerous to quarrel with mad people.

'There must be some mistake,' she said gently, 'your relation does not live here. I am quite alone in the house.'

She wished, the second after she had spoken, that she had not said this, because her visitor might be a burglar. He might be a mad burglar, and that would be worse than anything.

'Stands to reason he's here. I've been havin' a chat with him. There he is, look!'

Gummidge pointed a broomstick arm towards the hat-stand.

Things look different by moonlight when outlines are blurred, and shadows fall in strange places. The hat-stand, hung about as it was with human clothes, looked like a person.

'A gang!' screamed Mrs Bloomsbury-Barton, 'an armed gang!'

'Ooh aye!' replied Worzel Gummidge pleasantly, 'stands to reason I'm armed!'

Tripping over a mat, banging herself against a corner of the oak chest, Mrs Bloomsbury-Barton stumbled towards the door of the dining-room where the telephone was kept.

As she fumbled with the handle, she did not hear Worzel Gummidge muttering, 'Stands to reason I'm armed. A scarecrow as was only legged wouldn't be able to flap its coat sleeves at crows – not unless it wore the sleeves for trousies. Then it couldn't wave both legs at onest – not standin' up dignified.'

As Mrs Bloomsbury-Barton went into the dining-room, he continued, 'It's enough to make anyone sulk. I only come up for a chat. I didn't start sulky like *you*.'

He prodded the hat-stand, leaned up against it, and closed his eyes.

'I'll out-sulk you if it takes all summer,' he said.

So Miss Dollit found him when, swinging her hurricane lantern, she tripped into the hall.

'Mrs Bloomsbury-Barton!' she called, 'Mrs Bloomsbury-Barton, come and look!'

But Mrs Bloomsbury-Barton, who had fumbled for the telephone, and found it at last, groped for matches and found them, was dialling Scatterbrook 540, which was the number of the Policeman's house. It so happened that he was out. It was his evening off duty, and he had bicycled into Penfold to visit his aunt. The sister, with whom he shared his house, was rather deaf and very slow.

Mrs Bloomsbury-Barton was dialling frantically when Miss Dollit came into the dining-room.

'Thank goodness you've come, Phoebe,' she spoke in a hoarse whisper. 'Shut the door behind you, and lock it, *quickly*.'

'Lock it?' repeated Miss Dollit, 'but I want you to come and see the surprise. Kind Farmer Braithewaite —'

'LOCK THE DOOR!'

In her agitation Mrs Bloomsbury-Barton forgot to whisper and almost shouted, 'Will the Policeman never answer the telephone?'

'Policeman? Why do want the Policeman?'

Miss Dollit put down her lantern, and bumped against the door, so that it shut with a bang.

'Lock the door!' repeated Mrs Bloomsbury-Barton.

Miss Dollit looked guilty, and spoke apologetically.

'I'm afraid I can't do that. I meant to tell you, I borrowed the key to see if it would fit the woodshed door, and then I forgot to bring it back.'

A murmuring sounded from the telephone receiver, and Mrs Bloomsbury-Barton replied —

'Is that the Policeman? . . . No? . . . Oh, it's you, Miss Wilson. Please tell your brother I want him at once . . . I didn't say *bother*, I said BROTHER. . . . B for Bananas, R for Reggie . . . No, no, it isn't Reggie speaking! R for Reggie – BROTHER. I want your brother. I want the Policeman. . . . You say he's out? . . . He can't be out . . . There's a gang here . . . No, no, NO, not a *bang*, though there may be at any moment. . . . Not a bang – a *gang*. GANG. G for Gerty. No, Miss Wilson – it isn't Gerty speaking, it's —'

Suddenly, the room was flooded with light. Whatever was wrong with the electricity system had been put right.

Mrs Bloomsbury-Barton and Miss Dollit blinked at one another, and the voice from the Policeman's house continued
to murmur.

Mrs Bloomsbury-Barton answered it again. 'Telephone
to Penfold, Miss Wilson. Ask for a policeman to be sent at
once.'

She hung up the receiver.

'What *has* happened?' asked Miss Dollit. 'An armed
gang? I don't understand.'

'Did you come in through the back door?'

'No, through the front, and I was going to tell you —'

'Never mind that. Come quickly. We can lock ourselves
into a bedroom. We shall be safer upstairs until the police
come.'

Mrs Bloomsbury-Barton hurried to the door, opened it,
and whispered, 'On tip-toe, Phoebe, walk on tip-toe, and
don't make a sound!'

A voice – it seemed to come from the drawing-room on
the opposite side of the hall – spoke crisply, 'Break! Break!'

Another voice said, 'What a punch! It's hurt him. Yes,
it's hurt him badly. It's shaken him . . . his eyebrow's cut
again, but he's fighting back. What a punch! What a
punch!'

There was a pause.

'Now's our chance!' said Mrs Bloomsbury-Barton, 'they're
fighting among themselves. Come upstairs quickly.'

She led the way up the shallow flight of stairs, and Miss
Dollit followed. When they reached the half-landing, they
paused for breath, and looked down, and along the shining
banister rail to the hall below where Worzel Gummidge,
sulking still, lolled against the hat-stand.

'There they are,' gasped Mrs Bloomsbury-Barton, 'they've
stopped fighting.'

Miss Dollit peered over the rail.

'But that's Old Man Scarecrow!' she cried. 'I tried to

tell you that I found him in the hall. Farmer Braithewaite must have brought him.'

'There were two men,' quavered Mrs Bloomsbury-Barton uncertainly, 'I saw them quite – well *almost* distinctly. One was a great deal taller than the scarecrow.'

Certainly the hat-stand was a great deal taller than Worzel Gummidge who, still in a dead sulk, leaned against it.

'I couldn't have been mistaken? No, of course I couldn't. Besides they spoke to me, at least one of them *spoke*: he told me he was armed.'

The voice of the BBC commentator announced, 'Now we will return you to the studio. We will let you know the result of this light-heavyweight contest later on in the programme.'

There was a pause, and Miss Dollit cried triumphantly, 'You must have heard somebody speaking over the radio! We can hear it quite distinctly from here. We didn't turn it off when the lights went.'

For a moment Mrs Bloomsbury-Barton looked, as she felt, very foolish indeed.

Then it was her turn to triumph.

'Don't be ridiculous, Phoebe! How could the radio be *on* when the electricity was off?'

'I don't pretend to understand electricity, but if one can believe in radio one can believe in anything.'

Worzel Gummidge stirred slightly, and spoke in his sulk, 'Don't talk so daft! Stands to reason! OOH AYE.'

'There's a play on the radio!' said Miss Dollit, 'let's go into the drawing-room, and listen.'

But Mrs Bloomsbury-Barton clung to the banisters and said, 'I would rather stay here where I am until the police come.'

'Then you'll have to stay here all night,' Miss Dollit giggled provokingly. 'Yes, you'll have to stay here all night because you didn't give your name or address to poor Miss Wilson. She thinks you are Gerty or Reggie!'

Mrs Bloomsbury-Barton glared at her. Worzel Gummidge smiled in his sulk, but nobody noticed the smile.

# 4 The Lamb in the Orchard

Even Miss Dollit was beginning to find the pet lamb just a little bit of a nuisance. It followed her everywhere – even into the kitchen, though Mrs Marble threatened to 'walk out' every time she saw it.

'I've had more than enough to do, thank *you*,' she said, 'I've had more than enough to do, wearing my fingers to the bone elbow-greasing that hat-stand without rubbing lambs' nose-marks from the kitchen table legs. You never saw such a state as the meogany was in – all scratches as well as smears.' (She had not seen Worzel Gummidge, who had been put into the greenhouse until Miss Dollit needed him for her tea-garden, and so she blamed the lamb for the damage done by the scarecrow's boots and twiggy fingers.)

'You couldn't think anything that looks so soft could scratch like that. It must have made them with its nasty little hooves. And jump, I'll say it can jump! Some of the marks were as high as my head. It'll take weeks to get that meogany back to what it was.'

At lunch-time, the lamb bleated pathetically just outside the dining-room window. At tea-time, it pushed its soft nose against the french window of the drawing-room, opened its mouth, and baa-ed incessantly. In fact, it was seldom quiet when Miss Dollit was out of sight.

The lamb pranced among the crocuses, and danced on the daffodils.

'It likes flowers better than grass!' explained Miss Dollit

when Dodgson, the gardener, objected. 'It likes pretty things.'

'There won't be much for it to like soon,' grunted the gardener, 'not in the flower-beds or in the greenhouse. It must have been there most of Sunday, jumping about on the staging. Just you come and look.'

Miss Dollit followed him, saying as she went, that the lamb had spent its Sunday with her except for an hour when she was in church.

'It did a lot in an hour then,' grunted the gardener, as he opened the greenhouse door.

Worzel Gummidge was propped against the staging at the far end. Boxes which should have been green with the young leaves of seedlings – stocks, pansies, polyanthus and dwarf dahlias – were littered with the uprooted plants.

'But the lamb couldn't jump as high as that!' said Miss Dollit, and the lamb, which had followed her into the greenhouse, gave a protesting baa.

'Mrs Marble says it's a rare jumper!' replied the gardener. 'She's suffered from its high jumps.'

There was a rustle of straw from the other end of the greenhouse.

'Stands to reason!' muttered Worzel Gummidge amiably, 'as no lamb as wasn't daft'd demean itsel' to eat flowers – nasty fiddlin' little things. Grass is better than flowers.'

Miss Dollit stared at the gardener, who was trying, with the greatest tenderness, to push some thread-like roots back into the earth. It was well known in Scatterbrook that Mr Dodgson loved flowers as devotedly as mother birds love their fledgelings.

'What did you say?' she asked.

The gardener did not answer. He seldom replied to questions when he was doing any work that needed care. Some people said that he could not, and others that he would not hear.

'Well!' said Miss Dollit, and, picking up the lamb, she left Worzel Gummidge and the gardener alone together.

Nearly a week went by. During that time Worzel Gummidge enjoyed the longest sulk of his life in the greenhouse, Earthy Mangold had the longest weep of her life in Miss Dollit's orchard, Robin made two new sardine-tin shoes for Mildew Turmut, and carried her back to the railway allotment.

Every day, the lamb became more and more unpopular with everyone in Mrs Bloomsbury-Barton's house, and with the workmen who were making the ornamental pool in Miss Dollit's garden. This was because, like the lamb in the nursery rhyme, the little creature followed its owner everywhere.

'I shall call it Mary!' said Miss Dollit, 'yes, I shall call it Mary after the rhyme –

> "Everywhere that Mary went,
> The lamb was sure to go."'

'But your name is NOT Mary,' objected Mrs Bloomsbury-Barton.

'I know, but it's too late to change *my* name, and the lamb needs one. I'll find it now. I shall very soon teach it to come running when I call.'

'But it comes running without your calling,' objected Mrs Bloomsbury-Barton. 'Do, PLEASE, if you are going into the garden, shut the front door behind you. Mrs Marble is in one of her very worst moods. I dread to think what may happen if that lamb comes into the hall again.'

'Mary! Mary!' cried Miss Dollit as she hurried across the lawn. 'Mary!' she cried as she reached the back door, 'Mary! Mary! Mary!'

Now, it so happened that the lamb had discovered a bowl full of potato-peelings, cabbage stalks, tea-leaves, coffee-grounds, porridge and the scrapings from burned toast. This had been left on the back door step to be collected by the milkman, who kept pigs. The lamb was having a most glorious time.

'Mary!' repeated Miss Dollit, and now she almost yodelled the word, 'Mary! Mary!' The door was flung open.

'I'm coming as fast as I can!' said Mrs Marble. 'Oh, it's you, is it, Miss Dollit? I thought it was the milkman!'

The lamb raised its happy face from the pig-bowl. A long strand of apple-peeling dangled from its left ear, and its nose was splattered with porridge and coffee-grounds.

'MARY!' exclaimed Miss Dollit, 'how naughty you are!'

Mrs Marble spoke slowly, 'The milkman, seeing he's my own brother-in-law, calls me Mary. So does my husband when the fit takes him, but I'm Mrs Marble to the rest of the world. I'll thank you to remember that, Miss Dollit.'

The lamb danced on its stubby legs, sending the rubbish flying over the flagstones.

'But I call the lamb *Mary*,' explained poor Miss Dollit, 'I call her *Mary* because —'

The lamb skipped towards Mrs Marble. Lovingly, or perhaps because it had no handkerchief, it rubbed its grubby little face on the spotless apron, rubbed again, and bleated 'Maa! Maa!'

'I'll have no lamb called after me,' said Mrs Marble. 'I'll put my hat on now, and I'll not take it off again in this house.'

Miss Dollit almost bleated, 'I could call it by another name.'

'You can call it what you like,' replied Mrs Marble. 'I shan't be here to hear, nor to clean the doorstep after it.'

Untying her apron, she turned back to the kitchen. Miss Dollit followed, and so did the lamb. Mrs Bloomsbury-Barton, who had forgotten to tell Mrs Marble that Captain Conway was expected to lunch, was standing by the kitchen table.

Mrs Marble told her story, Miss Dollit tried to explain what had happened, while the lamb butted in, and bleated happily.

'That's what I said, and that's what I mean!' ended Mrs Marble, and she jerked her hat from its peg. 'I'll not share my kitchen nor my name with a nasty little creature like that!'

She slammed on her hat, and pointed towards the lamb, who had discovered a tin of black boot polish, danced in it, and was printing hoof marks on the red linoleum.

'But Mrs Marble,' Mrs Bloomsbury-Barton spoke despairingly, 'what shall we do without you?'

'That's not for me to say.' Mrs Marble took off her apron and rolled it into a bundle. 'You may find *someone* willing to share a kitchen with a lamb, but I'll be surprised if you do. Anyone that likes to share with a lamb won't give much thought or elbow-grease to the meogany.'

'The lamb must go!' announced Mrs Bloomsbury-Barton. 'You must find a new home for it, Phoebe.'

'I don't say,' – Mrs Marble stopped fastening her coat – 'I don't say that if the creature goes, I mightn't stay on, just for a bit. You can take your choice between the two of us unless you happen to fancy *roast lamb*!'

The idea was so horrible to Miss Dollit that she stooped down, picked up the lamb, and hugged it very hard indeed.

'Then that's all settled,' said Mrs Bloomsbury-Barton. 'Take that creature away, Phoebe, there's no reason why it should not stay in your own orchard at *The Treasure Ship*. Now, Mrs Marble, we must have a specially nice lunch today for Captain Conway, mustn't we? Everything is settled quite nicely now.'

But Miss Dollit as, followed by the lamb, she hurried towards *The Treasure Ship* knew that nothing was settled. She was quite sure that the lamb would not stay in an unfenced orchard unless she stayed with it.

Farmer Braithewaite was coming out of the Post Office, and Miss Dollit told her sad story to him.

'I know Mrs Braithewaite wouldn't think of taking it back,' he said, 'but I've been thinking of my niece up in Cumberland —'

'But that's such a long journey!' interrupted Miss Dollit.

'I wasn't thinking of journeys,' explained Farmer Braithewaite, 'I was thinking how my niece took a fancy to a lamb, and how the lamb took a fancy to her. She was in the Women's Land Army at the time, and the lamb followed her about same as this one follows you. The trouble was she'd taken on the cowman's job. The lamb made it awkward at milking-time, if you see what I mean?'

Miss Dollit nodded.

'The lamb wouldn't leave the milking pails alone. It wasn't so much what it drank as what it jumped in. It was in and out of the pails like a wild-cat, and when it grew bigger it started tipping them over until the farmer said it must go. You couldn't blame him, could you?'

Again Miss Dollit shook her head. She did not exactly blame Mrs Bloomsbury-Barton either, but that fact was not making the morning any easier.

'My niece was a grand girl. She wouldn't be beat by anything. She made a scarecrow, and she dressed it up in her pull-on hat, and old green jumper and Land Army breeches. Then she set it up in a meadow, and let the lamb go along with it. She'd no more trouble after that. The lamb took to the scarecrow same as it took to my niece, and left her free for the milking. See what I mean? Now you've a scarecrow in that orchard of yours. See what I mean?'

'Yes,' agreed Miss Dollit, 'but I'm not a Land-girl. I mean I don't wear breeches.'

'Bless you!' The farmer broke into a cackling laugh. 'It's not the shape of what you wear: it's the smell. See what I mean?'

He pointed towards the lamb, who was now nuzzling and mumbling the edge of Miss Dollit's pleated skirt.

'Animals go by smell. How else would a kitten turn to its mother before its eyes were open? How else'd a new-born lamb know its own mother from the flock? There's not all that variation in sheep's faces. It's the smell of your clothes that attracts the lamb, Miss Dollit, and no offence meant.'

'Oh!' exclaimed Miss Dollit, 'WHAT an idea!'

She pushed past the farmer, and the lamb followed trippingly. Mr Braithewaite raised his voice, 'When I said *smell* I should have said *scent*, considering I was speaking to a lady. SCENT like foxes have when hounds are following. I never meant to offend you.'

Miss Dollit was not offended. She was happier than she had been since breakfast-time, but she was in a hurry.

'Now I've said the wrong thing,' muttered the farmer. 'Well, I dunno!'

Nobody, except Mrs Kibbins's cat, who was sharpening her claws on the top of a lichen-trimmed wall, heard him. Miss Dollit and the lamb were hurrying into the orchard where Earthy Mangold stood forlornly under an apple-tree.

Deserted by Worzel Gummidge, the little scarecrow was thinking her kind but muddled thoughts. The bottle-straw boots that had been so bright and golden were broken and bent because she had given bits of them to nest-building sparrows. She had, hoping to save trouble to some weary bird, built a clumsy little nest of twigs, grass and mud in the fork of an overhanging bough, but no bird sat in it. She had over-turned one or two up-turned beetles, and sung a lullaby to a homing pigeon. The beetles had scuttled away, the pigeon had taken no notice, and poor little Earthy Mangold was forlorn.

The green tears had dried on her cheeks long before Miss Dollit found her. Now she was doing her very best to sulk in memory of Worzel Gummidge, who had sulked so long and so often.

'Let me see,' said Miss Dollit, who had a habit of speaking her thoughts aloud, 'let me think. If I give you my clothes, I shall have to go home in SOMETHING because your things wouldn't fit me.'

She glanced at Earthy's sacking cloak and skirt, bottle-straw boots, basket hat, and the checked apron from whose pocket a banana-skin handkerchief peeped out.

The scarecrow opened one eye, and noticed Miss Dollit's fawn pleated skirt, pink cardigan and jumper, and the blue headscarf with its printed design of flowers and splodges. It was difficult to keep on sulking, but she closed the eye again.

'Let me see,' repeated Miss Dollit. 'Yes, I know! I left my old macintosh in *The Treasure Ship*.'

She hurried away, and the lamb followed her.

Quarter-of-an-hour later, the little creature was gazing in a puzzled way from one strange-looking figure to another.

Miss Dollit, bare-legged, bare-headed, and wearing a button-less macintosh over a pink petticoat, *looked* all right as seen through a lamb's eyes, but the smell of her clothes was unfamiliar. The reek of macintosh and paint (for Miss Dollit had helped to decorate *The Treasure Ship*, and was not very handy with a brush) were not friendly.

The lamb bleated sadly, and skipped towards Earthy Mangold. The little creature was wearing a pleated skirt, so much too long for her that the hem frilled on the grass. The empty feet of a pair of brown stockings lay limply beyond the hem. This was because Earthy's hawthorn-bough legs were too short for grown-up stockings. The headscarf hid half of her sprouting hair, and the sleeves of the jumper almost covered her twiggy fingers. She wore the cardigan as a cloak, for Miss Dollit had been in a hurry, and it is not easy to dress a stiffly-jointed scarecrow.

The lamb was not fussy about fashions.

It bounded on to the pleated skirt.

'Ma-aa!' it bleated lovingly, 'Ma-aa! Ma-aa!'

Miss Dollit left it alone with Earthy. Because the macintosh had no buttons, she clutched it round her, and hurried back to the White House.

Mrs Bloomsbury-Barton was in the hall; so was Captain Conway, who had arrived rather early for lunch.

'How do you do?' he said, glancing at the paint-splashed, distemper-smeared macintosh. 'I can see you've had a busy morning's decorating. It's wonderful what women do nowadays.'

'I'll just run upstairs and make myself tidy,' murmured Miss Dollit.

'Please, Phoebe, leave that macintosh in the porch.' Mrs Bloomsbury-Barton spoke very firmly. 'You know the smell of paint always gives me a headache.'

'Then I'll put it in the toolshed,' said Miss Dollit.

Captain Conway stepped forward as she darted towards the front door.

'Let me take it,' he said, 'I insist!'

'No! No! No!' Miss Dollit yelled as she tugged at the door-knob. 'I can manage. I know where the shed is.'

The toolshed was in the shrubbery. So, too, propped against a lilac bush, was Worzel Gummidge, who had been put there by the gardener after tidying the greenhouse.

The scarecrow was in a dead sulk, and Miss Dollit did not notice him as she whisked into the shed.

It would be easy enough to leave the macintosh there, but how (bare-legged and in a very short pink petticoat) could she hope to pass the French windows of the drawing-room without being noticed by Mrs Bloomsbury-Barton or Captain Conway?

She looked about her. There, hanging on a peg, was the gardener's new overcoat. As a rule he only wore an overcoat on Sundays, but today he had planned to go to Dimden when his work was done. A green woollen muffler hung on another peg.

*I could borrow the coat, and put it back directly after lunch,* thought Miss Dollit. *I can slip through the kitchen, and go up the back stairs. Then Mrs Bloomsbury-Barton can't ask tiresome questions because she won't see me.*

The trouble was that Mrs Bloomsbury-Barton had given the pink cardigan and jumper to Miss Dollit as a Christmas present, and would be annoyed for them to have been lent to a scarecrow.

Mrs Marble, who was dishing-up the luncheon, gave Miss Dollit a long and suspicious stare as she hurried through the kitchen.

There was peace in the White House until half-past two in the afternoon.

Miss Dollit, wearing a brown jumper and brown pleated skirt, had managed to return the gardener's coat to the shed. She was sitting in the drawing-room with Mrs Bloomsbury-Barton and Captain Conway when Mrs Marble opened the door.

'Yes, you can take the coffee cups,' said Mrs Bloomsbury-Barton. 'I expect you would like to finish washing-up.'

Mrs Marble pounced on the tray, and stalked towards the door. Then, looking up at the ceiling, she said, 'Mr Dodgson's knocking off work early because he's got to catch the bus to Dimden.'

'Yes, of course, that's quite all right,' said Mrs Bloomsbury-Barton, 'he told me about it.'

'If Miss Dollit's finished with his overcoat, Mr Dodgson would like it back.' Mrs Marble continued to speak to a fly on the ceiling. 'Miss Dollit must have taken it from the shed.'

'DID you, Phoebe?' asked Mrs Bloomsbury-Barton.

'Yes, but I only borrowed it, and only just for lunch – I mean only just before lunch, and when I'd put the macintosh in the shed.'

'Why?' asked Mrs Bloomsbury-Barton, 'It was not a cold morning.'

'It wasn't because of the cold,' said Miss Dollit, 'it was because of having to change clothes because of the lamb.'

'If,' Mrs Marble glared at Mrs Bloomsbury-Barton, 'if that lamb's had anything to do with Mr Dodgson's overcoat, I don't suppose he'll fancy it again, any more than I fancied my apron this morning. After all, aprons do B O I L.'

'But I put it back – the overcoat, I mean,' cried poor Miss Dollit, 'I put it back just before lunch.'

Mrs Marble ignored her, and turned to Mrs Bloomsbury-Barton.

'The coat's not in the shed now. I've looked with my own eyes. It was before lunch I saw Miss Dollit wearing it when she slipped through the kitchen.'

'Tell Dodgson I'll see him presently,' said Mrs Bloomsbury-Barton.

'He's got to go early to catch the Dimden bus.'

Balancing the tray on one knee, Mrs Marble opened the door, and then stumped out into the drawing-room.

'Perhaps it would help if I had a word with Dodgson?' suggested Captain Conway. 'Of course there's been some silly mistake. We'll unravel the mystery between us.' (Miss Dollit gave a little shudder.) 'We used to play cricket together in the old days. He captained the Scatterbrook Eleven when I was a little chap. We were great pals in those days.' He smiled kindly at Miss Dollit. 'I'll remind him of our old cricketing days.'

'I don't see how *games* can help,' snapped Mrs Bloomsbury-Barton.

Mr Dodgson did not look eager to play games as he shuffled along the path that led to the shed.

'That coat was there at noon, and it was gone by two o'clock – so was the muffler,' he muttered.

'Remember those sixes you used to hit, Dodgson?' asked Captain Conway. 'Remember teaching me to bowl?'

'It was gone by two o'clock,' repeated the gardener.

'Remember how you took seven wickets the first year we played Dimden?' asked Captain Conway.

'My pipe was in my pocket – my pipe AND baccy. It was eight wickets I took.'

'I'll buy you a new pipe,' said Miss Dollit miserably, 'a new pipe and a new overcoat. I didn't borrow the muffler.'

Mr Dodgson grunted unbelievingly.

'Remember how you caught the Vicar out?' asked Captain Conway.

Mrs Bloomsbury-Barton opened the door of the shed. Neither coat, muffler nor macintosh hung from any of the rusty nails.

'See what I said!' The gardener jerked a muddy thumb towards the empty wall. 'The coat and muffler was gone by two o'clock, same as I said. I've got to catch the bus to Dimden.'

'WELL, Phoebe?' asked Mrs Bloomsbury-Barton.

Miss Dollit, who had darted to the window, replied in a series of little shrieks – 'Look! Look! Look!'

She continued to shriek as the others peeped over her shoulders. With his back towards them, and facing the lilac bush, stood Worzel Gummidge. His broomstick arms stood straight out from his shoulders. The gardener's coat dangled from his right wrist, Miss Dollit's macintosh draped his left arm, the green muffler hung from his shoulders, and a piece of sacking covered his hat.

'A tramp, by George!' shouted Captain Conway as, followed by the others, he dashed out of the shed.

'It's only Old Man Scarecrow. Don't spoil him!' pleaded Miss Dollit.

'Spoil him? I'll teach the fellow the lesson of his life!'

There was a creaking and rustling. The smell of paint and turnip mingled in the spring air.

'Well, I'm jiggered!' Captain Conway, his hands full of coats and muffler and sacking, stared at Worzel Gummidge's shabby back. 'He – it – looked like a tramp.'

The scarecrow coughed his sheep-like cough, but only Miss Dollit noticed the slight stir of the stuffing under the shabby coat, and the jerky movement of the broomstick arms.

'He looks as though he's shivering!' she cried.

Another cough answered her, and Captain Conway turned to the gardener. 'You'd better put your coat on,' he said, 'we can't have you coughing like that.'

'Did you hang those things on the scarecrow, Phoebe?' asked Mrs Bloomsbury-Barton.

Miss Dollit shook her head, and another voice answered for her – 'Stands to reason a hat-stand's got to dress like a hat-stand! Ooh aye!'

Mrs Bloomsbury-Barton glanced sharply at the two men, but Captain Conway was shaking out the macintosh, and the gardener was fumbling in his overcoat pockets.

'Pipe's gone!' he muttered. 'It was there at twelve o'clock time.'

Miss Dollit found the pipe, which was caught in the twigs of the lilac bush above Worzel Gummidge's head.

'Well! Well!' said Captain Conway. 'So you're all right now, Dodgson, aren't you? D'you know the sight of that old scarecrow with all those coats slung round him took me back to times when we played cricket on the green. Remember how old Fred liked to be umpire, and how we hung our jackets on him?'

The gardener nodded as he filled his pipe. Captain Conway lit it for him as he continued to chat. 'Poor old Fred! He *would* be umpire even when his sight was failing, and he couldn't see the ball a yard away. He said he liked to hear the crack when you sent a ball to boundary. Those were the days, eh, Dodgson?'

The gardener answered between puffs of his pipe. 'Those were the days! Baccy doesn't smoke like it did. This stuff might be turnip parings.'

## 5 The Statue of a Lamb

Earthy Mangold was happier than she had been for many days. She was proud of her new clothes and her new occupation, and prouder still of the lamb.

'I'm a shepherd now,' she told Upsidaisy, the educated scarecrow who had trundled up from the school allotments to visit her friend.

'A shepherd's a *he*,' corrected Upsidaisy. 'Seein' as you're a *she*, you'll have to be a shepherdess. We learns that in grammar.'

'It won't make no differ.' Earthy looked lovingly at the lamb, who was wearing one of Miss Dollit's stockings as a muffler. 'I'll love Mary-love just the same.'

'It do make a differ!' Upsidaisy, who had three milking-stool legs and had lost one of her socks, and grudged the lamb its use of the stocking, did not speak very kindly. 'You're dressed all wrong for a shepherdess.'

'Oh, Upsidaisy, *love*!' cried Earthy, 'Miss Dollit dressed me most partikcler for the lamb. Look at me grand skirt all pleated up like musheroom underneaths!'

'Little Bo Peep were a shepherdess. The childers says po'try about her. I've heard 'em when I've lurked under the school winders.'

'Were she a scarecrow same as me?' asked Earthy anxiously.

'She were Norma from school when she weren't Bo Peep, and all dressed up at the school concert. She were dressed in blue sating.'

'What's sating?' asked Earthy.

'It's blue like sky-stuff but it's all shiny like when snails've been crawlin' over slates. The blue sating dress were all bunched up at the sides.'

(Earthy tugged at her pleated skirt, and tried to pull it into bunches.)

'AND she'd a shawl like cobwebs round her neck!'

Earthy raised her head – there *was* a rather dingy shred of cobweb caught between her neck and Miss Dollit's jumper. Upsidaisy glanced at it, and continued, 'Bo Peep's shawl were *white*, and she showed a pink sating petticoat each side where the blue sating dress were bunched up.' (Earthy pulled the skirt higher, but showed nothing grander than some rags of sacking.) 'AND she'd a straw hat with pink roses and dangles o' blue ribbin hangin' down the back.'

Earthy glanced towards the jumble of her old clothes lying on the grass where Miss Dollit had left them. The brim of the basket hat was frayed because the lamb had been sampling the taste of straw.

'It's too early for roses,' she said sadly.

Upsidaisy continued her list of grandeurs.

'Bo Peep had mittens.'

'What's mittens?' asked Earthy humbly.

'Mittens is what kittens wear. There's a pome about 'em as you'd know if you was eddicate.'

Upsidaisy chanted in a schoolchild's voice –

> 'Three little kittens
> Once lost their mittens.'

'I've never seen cats nor kittens in anything but their own furs,' argued Earthy.

'That's acos they'd lost their mittens same as in the pome,' said Upsidaisy triumphantly. 'Bo Peep sang a pome about hersel' at the school concert. It started –

"I'm little Bo Peep,
    I've lost my sheep,
    I don't know where to find 'em.'"

'Beggin' your pardon,' interrupted Earthy, 'beggin' your pardon, and if it's all the same to you, if I lost lamb-love, I'd know where to find her.'

Upsidaisy, determined to show off her knowledge, took no notice, but went on with her story – 'When Bo Peep finished singin' all the other childers at the concert shouted –

"Leave 'em alone,
    And they'll come home,
    Bringin' their tails behind 'em.'"

'And where else'd they wear 'em?' Kind little Earthy sounded almost cross. 'They wouldn't look purty with their tails hangin' down over their faces.'

'Stands to reason they'd not look so daft as they does now!' announced Worzel Gummidge, who had just shambled into the orchard. 'Tails is for whiskin' flies away, and flies allus settles on faces. Time and again, I seen horses and cows in the medders with their faces black with flies, and their tails whiskin' away at their back ends. If they wore their tails in front they could flick the flies out o' their eyes. Stands to reason.'

Upsidaisy smiled up at him. She admired Worzel Gummidge very much. The lamb waggled its own tail joyfully, bunched its hooves together, and jumped on to a mole-hill.

With one broomstick leg Gummidge stirred the little heap of Earthy's clothes. Then he gathered them up, and shook and jerked himself about until the cloak and skirt were spread over his outstretched arms. The basket hat dangled from one wrist, and the string of the apron was twisted round the only button of his coat.

'I'll show 'em I knows how to dress like a hat-stand,' he muttered. 'They took the gardener's clothes off o' me, but they'll not get these.'

'Oh, Worzel, love,' cried Earthy, 'casn't you give over bein' hat-stand and turn back to husbin?'

'I don't know as hat-stands does give over bein' hat-stands. I don't know as they ever does turn back to husbins.'

A trickle of green tears ran down Earthy Mangold's cheeks, and she sobbed, 'I don't know as shepherdess can turn back to wife neither. Go on learnin' me to be a shepherdess, Upsidaisy, love.'

'I've learned you all there is to learn,' said Upsidaisy, gazing at Worzel Gummidge as he shambled out of the orchard and towards the summer-house. 'You've got to wear sating and roses and bunched up skirts and mittens what the kittens lost, and you've got to learn to leave sheep alone else they'll grow their tails in front.'

Earthy looked anxiously at the lamb, so as to make quite certain that its tail was in the proper place.

'It doesn't sound a busy workin' life,' she said. 'Casn't I do nothin' else?'

'You've got to carry a crooked stick with a bunch o' blue ribbins tied round the crook,' Upsidaisy told her. 'You need it for hooking the lambs back if they falls down wells or gets stuck in mud or caught in brambles.'

Earthy looked round the safe and sunny orchard and across to a fallen tree trunk which the lamb was trying to climb.

'If it winds that stockin' round a bough it'll maybe hang itsel' and you with no crook to hook it back by,' added Upsidaisy. 'That stocking'd be safer round my bare leg than worn as a muffler round the lamb's neck, and you with no crook to hook it back by.'

'Beggin' your pardon, and if it's all the same to you, that stockin' was give to my leg by Miss Dollit.'

'Keep it an' welcome!' replied Upsidaisy generously, 'but

don' blame me if the lamb takes the stockin' off of you again and swallers it, and winds it round its heart and chokes itsel', and you with no crook to hook it back by. I've heard the teacher talkin' to the childers in sewin' class. "Never bite off cotton ends," she says. "If you bites off cotton ends and swallers 'em they'll wind theirsel's round your hearts and choke 'em." Stockin's is longer nor cotton ends and stronger and they easier wound —'

'You take it, Upsidaisy, love,' begged Earthy, 'you take it quick afore lamb-love starts to swaller.'

Upsidaisy trundled towards the lamb and soon her hands (they were woollen gloves stuffed with paper) were busily unwinding the stocking from the lamb's neck, and winding it round her own uncovered milking-stool leg.

'I'll be goin' now,' she said. 'Maybe Mr Gummidge'd like some company.' She pushed her way through the gap in the hedge that divided orchard from garden.

Worzel Gummidge, still draped in Earthy's old clothes, had propped himself against the summer-house.

'I thought maybe you'd like a bit o' company,' said Upsidaisy, as she trundled up to him.

'I don't know as hat-stands wants company,' muttered Worzel Gummidge. 'The one I met were sulkin'. Leave me be to enjoy a good sulk.'

He closed his eyes, and stiffened his broomstick limbs, so Upsidaisy trundled into the summer-house. At least, she would be near to hand to keep him company when he came out of his sulk. She looked through the dusty window, and saw Robin and Marlene Snooks.

Now it happened that the workmen had been given a day's holiday because the load of crazy-paving which they were to lay in the tea-garden was not due to arrive until the next day. Heaps of dry sand, cement and fine gravel stood ready for mixing, and Robin was busy with a spade and a bucket of water. Marlene was giving orders but

Upsidaisy could not hear the words.

'Make it nice and sloppy, Robin, or it'll set too quick and too thick and won't show the faces. We can always give them another dip if the fur shows through.'

Behind Marlene was a big cardboard carton which was stuffed to the brim with the old Christmas presents of many a Scatterbrook toddler.

Marlene had spent a happy morning collecting plush ducks and rabbits, cuddly dolls, monkeys, glove-puppets, and a woolly coated lamb on a wooden stand. She had not exactly *taken* them from their owners, but, as everybody knows, a toddler will usually drop what it is grasping and hold out its hands for anything new that may be offered.

Marlene had filled the outstretched hands of toddlers with old tennis balls, broken mechanical toys, curtain rings, rattles, tins of paint and other oddments from the store of junk she kept in her father's loft.

It happened that no mothers were there when the exchanges took place, so she had hurried to Finch Cottage where Robin was 'minding' his two-year-old sister in the garden. Marlene told her plan, and showed her treasures.

'If we dip them all in wet concrete and let them dry, we can sell them to Miss Dollit to go with the gnomes in the tea-garden. My Aunty Win has stone rabbits and squirrels and all sorts round the bird-bath on her rockery.'

'Why?' asked Robin.

'To look pretty, of course. Miss Dollit'll like them if she likes gnomes and toadstools. The workmen aren't working today. You come along and help me, and then Miss Dollit'll give me lots of money for all the stone animals.'

'*And* me?' asked Robin, who was very poor indeed that week because he had spent his pocket-money on a paint-box.

'They aren't your things,' objected Marlene. 'You could bring old Teddy, though.' She pointed to where the Teddy

Bear, legs and arms pointing skywards, lay on a patch of grass. 'Old Teddy would make a fine gnome.'

Robin looked doubtful. The Teddy Bear had been the sharer of his very young days. It had bald patches, and a long cut stitched with black cotton by his mother. It had a scorch-mark on its left ear, and a splodge of red ink on its tummy. Every mark was the reminder of some early adventure. Besides, it had been his only companion on his first exciting journey down to Scatterbrook. Earthy Mangold had mothered it, and called it 'Thing-Love'; it had taken its rightful place in the Scarecrow's Zoo, he had rescued it from the coke-dump, his kind Aunt Ruby had polished its bell, and tied a new ribbon round its neck.

'NO!' said Robin firmly.

'Why ever not?'

'It's history – sort of.'

'I never knew you were so set on history. You don't get many marks for it in school. You were bottom of the class last time!' jeered Marlene. 'You only want the bear 'cos you're a baby – a silly little baby boy. That's what it is.'

'No!' said Robin furiously, and his face went crimson under his very red hair. 'No, it's not that.'

'What is it then?' asked Marlene.

How could Robin explain that he loved the bear still, and that not for what it was, but for what it had been, for the sake of the scars that reminded him of his own short history as surely as the dints on old battle-axes can revive ancient wars to historians.

His little sister toddled towards him, staggered, and clutched at his hand to save herself from a tumble. The sight of her pink cheeks, the feel of her warmly grabbing fingers, gave Robin his excuse.

'The Teddy belongs to her now,' he said triumphantly, 'it belongs to Mary Lou.'

'Mary Lou! Mary Lou!' repeated his sister.

'A lot she cares for it!' snapped Marlene, who *knew* that the Teddy Bear would make the most wonderful gnome. 'Give her something else instead!'

'But what?' asked Robin.

'Wait! I'll show you!' Marlene turned round, and scrabbled in the carboard carton. From among the dolls and cuddly toys she pulled up an electric torch. Its battery had been 'dead' since long before Christmas but it was bright and shining, and just the right size for small fingers to grip.

She held it out to Robin's little sister.

'There you are!' she said as Mary Lou grabbed it. 'She likes it better than that old Teddy. I knew she would.'

'But,' explained poor Robin, 'Mum said that when Mary Lou grows up to be a Mother or when I grow up to be a Father, the Teddy will belong to our children.'

'A fine father you'll make if you don't know what children like to play with!' replied Marlene. 'Look at her now, and see what she likes best!'

Mary Lou was stumping round and round the Teddy Bear, but she was not looking at it. She was laughing for joy as she shook the torch until the battery made bumping noises inside it. She had found that the switch made little clicking noises, too.

She stumbled over the Teddy Bear, and squealed, 'Naughty old Ted!'

'What did I say?' repeated Marlene. 'Tell you what, we'll turn the old Teddy into a gnome, and if Mary Lou wants it again, we'll crack off the concrete easy as shelling an egg.'

'The concrete will stick to its fur,' objected Robin.

'Not if we oil it first,' said Marlene. 'When my Mum makes nougat, she oils the tin first and then none of the sweet stuff sticks when it's dry. I don't care though. I can manage by myself, and sell all the rabbits and ducks and things to Miss Dollit. Then I'll have money to go for a trip on the bus that's going I-know-where next week, and you won't! I don't care! Stay at home and play with your old Teddy. I know how to mix concrete.'

Her last words decided Robin. He loved mixing concrete. It made such a nice slushy noise as the spade chopped into it.

'There's a tin of dad's bike oil in the wash-house,' he said.

So that is how it was that Upsidaisy, from her hiding-place in the shrubbery, fluttered her paper-stuffed palms together in horror at what she saw.

When the concrete-pie (so beautifully like a mud-pie in feel and sloshiness) was mixed into the right kind of heap, Marlene grabbed a plush monkey from the carton.

'I'll do the first dip!' she said.

(Upsidaisy saw the little girl's lips moving, and pressed her own face closer to the dusty window-pane so that she could see more clearly.)

'Yes, I'll do the first dip,' she repeated, 'that's only fair as it's my monkey.'

(As a matter of fact, the monkey belonged to Clifford, who was Norma's two-year-old brother, and he was crying for it.)

'Twiddle its tail a bit more,' urged Robin as Marlene plunged the monkey into the wet concrete, and swirled it round.

'You'd better curl its tail a bit, too,' he added as the monkey, shedding blobs of concrete, was hauled up from the pie. 'If you don't curl it's tail, it will set like a poker. Monkeys use their tails to cling round trees. I've seen them at the Zoo.'

By now he was enjoying himself. The Teddy Bear, so soaked in bicycle oil that its fur looked as dank and dishevelled as the coat of a rain-drenched rabbit, lay beside him. Soon it would be his turn to play another part in this glorious game.

'You can curl its tail,' said Marlene generously. 'Curl its

tail, and put it by that gnome. No! Put it on that bit of plank. If we leave it by the gnome Miss Dollit will think it's a surprise *present* – not a surprise to buy.'

Her hands were stiff with concrete, so she rubbed some of it off, and picked up an old pair of coal tongs from the carton. (Marlene was the kind of little girl who prepared herself for everything – at least for everything that had to do with the junk shop she hoped to own one day.) While she wondered whether to dip a cuddly doll or the lamb on the wooden stand, Robin arranged the monkey on the plank, curled its tail and stretched out its arms so that they would harden in the breeze.

Except for a few bits of fur sticking out through the concrete on its cheeks, and except for a bare patch on its shoulder from which the concrete had dripped too quickly, it looked quite like the statue of a monkey.

Marlene made her choice. Picking up the doll in the tongs, she swished it to and fro, up and down, in the concrete 'pie'.

In another few minutes it sat (a curious lumpy figure with one leg bulging and with thick concrete tears swelling slowly on its cheeks) on the bench beside the monkey.

Now it was Robin's turn to transform the Teddy Bear into a statue. He might have hesitated for longer if the bear had not looked so very peculiar that it seemed better to cover up its oily coat. In its present state, it was no fit companion for Mary Lou or for any other child. He gripped the tongs.

'Go on!' said Marlene, 'go on before the concrete stiffens. It'll come off later, as easy as shell comes off an egg. I've told you so. Then you can clean it up with turps, and it'll look as good as new.'

The boot-button eyes of the Teddy Bear stared up at Robin. Because of the oil, they looked shinier now than ever they had done before, and much, much more alive.

He remembered the many other times when the bear's eyes had been a comfort to him – when his ear had ached so badly, when he had returned from his first day at the London school, when his father had been ill and his mother had had no time to tell a good-night story.

'Hurry up!' said Marlene, 'I want to do the lamb next.'

Robin remembered how the Teddy Bear had seemed to wink at him many and many a time when his grandmother had repeated, over and over again, that present-day children were very much worse than any children had been in her young days.

The memories of past joys and sorrows shared with the bear crowded into his mind. He remembered the bottle of turpentine in the wash-house at Finch Cottage.

'I'll clean him up NOW!' he said. 'I'll get the turps. Don't you touch it till I come back.'

The oil from the Teddy Bear's coat – at least *some* of the oil – showed in dark patches on Robin's shorts as he ran out of the garden.

'Softie!' muttered Marlene, as she picked up the tongs and plonked the toy lamb (stand and all) on to the heap of concrete. She was much too interested in her work to notice that Upsidaisy had trundled out of the summer-house, and was tugging at Worzel Gummidge's outstretched arm. She had not known that any scarecrows were near.

The concrete was stiffening rapidly, and each tong-full settled into a grey curl on the lamb's dingy coat. It had been a particularly life-like toy, and so nearly as large as a newly-born lamb that Upsidaisy, naturally, was very upset indeed.

'Mr Gummidge! Mr Gummidge!' she whispered, 'do please come out o' your sulk, and take a bit o' notice.'

Slowly, very slowly, the scarecrow opened one eye, and muttered, 'I don't know as hat-stands does take notice.'

'But Marlene Snooks – her from my school – is dippin' a

lamb in all that stuff.'

'Ooh aye! Stands to reason sheep's got to be dipped once a year, and lambs could do with it.'

'But, Mr Gummidge, she's turning the lamb into a statute!' said poor little Upsidaisy.

'Things is allus bein' changed into tother things or changin' theirsel's into tother things. Spiders changes flies into dinners. Ducks changes worms into suppers. Tadpoles changes theirsel's into frogs. It's the way they goes on. I've seen 'em at it afore I were a hat-stand. I don't take no notice now. Bein' a hat-stand's a peaceful sort o' job.'

Gummidge closed his eye, and his turnip face settled back into sulkiness.

'But, Mr Gummidge, do please to take notice, else Marlene'll turn Earthy's lamb into a statute, and it won't jump about no more nor bleat nor waggle its tail. I've seen photygraphs o' statutes in the school dustbins, and there's a statute in the play-ground made in the shape o' the man that built the school. It's dressed in a stone jacket and stone waistcoat, and it's got a stone walkin' stick and a stone hat and a stone book. It's been standing still for years and years and years, and it don't open its eyes nor answer back, even when the childers snowballs it.'

'Stands to reason it's a good sulker!' muttered Gummidge.

'But what'll Earthy's lamb do if it gets statuted?' asked Upsidaisy.

'It'll stand still, same as you said,' replied Gummidge. 'Do 'un good to stand still for a change. That lamb's a deal too restless, allus gallivantin' about and jumpin' and wagglin' its tail.'

'We did ought to help poor Earthy look arter it, and keep it safe,' pleaded poor little Upsidaisy. 'Earthy's not eddicate like you an' me, and she's not dressed right for bein' a shepherdess.'

Worzel Gummidge half-opened his left eye, closed it again, and answered, 'I don't know as hat-stands looks arter anythin' asides hats and coats. Leave me be, I'm sulkin'.'

'Maybe when you comes to you'll find you've been turned into a statute, Mr Gummidge,' said Upsidaisy crossly.

'I don't know as there is any statutes o' hat-stands!'

The scarecrow's limbs stiffened, his stuffing rustled, and then there was silence as he settled himself into a long sulk.

# 6 Kind Miss Armitage

Marlene was very proud of her finished work. There stood the lamb, its chunky legs fixed firmly to the wooden stand, stiff curls of concrete clinging to its coat, and its tail as thick as a flue brush. True, one ear was much broader than the other. True, one leg was stouter than the other three. True, there was a slight hump on one shoulder – that was because the drying concrete had set so quickly. True, it had a double chin.

All the same, its shape was the shape of a lamb.

'It looks fine!' said Marlene to herself, 'it looks fine. I'll put it on the plank alongside the monkey. Miss Dollit will be so surprised, she'll give me almost anything!'

She clasped her hands underneath the lamb, and tugged hard. There followed a rather nasty splintery sound. This was because the wooden stand was imbedded in dry concrete. (The truth is that the children had used too little sand, too little gravel, and a great deal too much cement when they had mixed their mixture. Concrete hardens very quickly.)

Marlene stopped tugging, and glanced at the gnomes in their scarlet jackets and peaked caps. The monkey looked pale beside them, and so did the lamb.

*There's paint in Dad's workshop*, thought Marlene, *lots of paint – lots of half-used tins, and there's pink and grey undercoating, too. I could paint the concrete green, so the lamb would look as though it was standing on a mound of grass – (there's lots of green left over from painting Mrs Bloomsbury-Barton's porch). And I could paint the inside of the lamb's ears with pink undercoating, and whitewash its curls. I'll give the monkey a scarlet jacket (there's red paint over from Mrs Kibbins's fence) and I'll give it a red cap, too.*

She looked hesitatingly at the Teddy Bear. It would be fun to turn him into a statue before Robin's return, but the concrete was so stiff that some more would have to be mixed. Painting was fun. She prodded the Teddy Bear with her foot so that he fell backwards, and lolled against the lamb.

'You can just wait till I come back,' she said before turning to run out of the garden.

Upsidaisy heard the words, and knew that there was no time to lose. She trundled as quickly as she could into the orchard, where Earthy Mangold was gazing lovingly at the lamb.

It took quite a long time to tell the story. This was partly because Earthy sobbed so bitterly, and partly because the lamb had discovered that butting was great fun, and that the school scarecrow was not at all steady on her milking-stool legs. She grew so tired of being knocked down and struggling up again that she finished her tale on the ground while the lamb nibbled her socks.

'Marlene's got the Teddy Bear, too,' she said, 'she's got Teddy-Bear-Thing-Love that you was so fond of afore the lamb came along. She's goin' to statute it as well as the lamb.'

'Oh, Thing-love!' moaned Earthy, 'Oh, Lamb-love! How shall we save 'em?'

'You'll have to drive 'em up to the Downs. There used to be sheep and shepherds there oncst,' Upsidaisy told her.

'But Thing-love casn't walk, so he casn't be drove!' Earthy took two or three tottering steps but Miss Dollit's skirt was so much too long for her that she moved as slowly and awkwardly as the last runner in a sack-race.

'And I casn't walk proper neither,' she moaned, 'the skirt's too fond o' me feet. I'll never get up to the Downs.'

'You'll have to take your clothes off.'

Upsidaisy stretched out a rustling hand, gripped Earthy, and struggled to her own three feet. 'That's what you'll have to do.'

'But I'll not look like a shepherdess in me sticks and stuffin'!'

Upsidaisy looked shocked, and spoke severely. 'If you thinks more o' lookin' smart than you thinks of a innercent lamb bein' statuted, you did ought to be ashamed.'

'Beggin' your pardon, and if it's all the same to you, Lamb-love dotes on clothes more nor on me, and it wouldn't be drove if I went in me sticks and stuffin' acos it dotes on these clothes.'

'Let *it* wear the clothes then, and you go in your sticks and stuffin',' said Upsidaisy reasonably.

But Earthy Mangold shook her head so violently that some of her green tears were jerked on to Upsidaisy's cheeks.

'If Lamb-love wore the clothes, it'd only stand still admirin' and dotin' on itsel', and we'd not get nowheres. Oh, Upsidaisy, what can we do?'

The school scarecrow thought for a moment or two. Then she smiled, and clapped her paper-stuffed hands together so that they rustled like leaves in Autumn.

'We can go to the Cruelty Lady!' she cried. 'She'll know what to do with the lamb.'

'That's not a nice-soundin' name,' objected Earthy. 'It's a very unkind-soundin' name.'

'It's what the childers call her when she comes to the school, and tells 'em how to go on about animals. She's not lived in Scatterbrook no more nor a week. She used to live in Dimden but she often come to Scatterbrook School. She brings a little dog not so big as half a rat.'

Earthy interrupted indignantly. 'Then it did ought to be

comforted and fed proper till it swells to the right size.'

'It's a mock dog,' continued Upsidaisy, 'it's made o' wood and it's got a wooden plate in its paws, and the Cruelty Lady makes the childers put their pennies on the tray so's the dog can tip 'em into its kennel.'

'It don't sound kind nor nateral. Bones'd be better nor pennies.'

'The pennies is for other animals and birds and fishes and insecks that's been treated cruel,' said Upsidaisy. 'The childers calls her the Cruelty Lady but they did ought to call her the Uncruelty Lady. Her right name's Miss Armitage, and she lives in the new bunglehole alongside the Post Office.'

'What use is pennies to trod-on worms, or upside-down beetles, and slugs that's been swallered by ducks?' asked Earthy. 'They needs pullin' out and right-side-uppin' and comfortin'. They don't want to go shoppin'.'

'Maybe the Cruelty Lady does their shoppin' for 'em,' said Upsidaisy. 'Anyways she tell the childers to tell her if they sees other childers bird-nestin' or teasin' dogs. There was a swan that hurt its wing and sat down in a ploughed field. The Cruelty Lady's keeping it in the back-yard o' the bunglehole till it's better. I'm goin' to tell her about the lamb that's been statuted, seein' as I'm eddicate and belongs to the school. You can wait and let *your* lamb be statuted and go on bein' a mock shepherdess.'

'Ma-aa! Ma-aa!' bleated the lamb so determinedly that Earthy Mangold, stumbling over her pleated skirt, followed Upsidaisy. The lamb, of course, followed too.

Now, Miss Armitage, who was very kind indeed, and who did all kinds of dirty jobs in the morning, liked to have her bath in the afternoon. True, she washed her hands before lunch, but after she had walked through muddy lanes in winter, and along dusty roads in summer so that she could exercise dogs who would have had no walks but for her, she felt tired and grubby, and in need of a long soak in hot water. She had combed the tangles from the coats of neglected kittens. She had cleaned out the hen-houses belonging to people who were ill or were too lazy to bother about the welfare of fowls so long as the birds laid eggs for breakfast. She had bathed puppies' eyes, and washed the grit from between their paws. She had made sure that the rabbits, living in little back-yards, had fresh greenstuff and were shaded from the sun when their owners were visiting Dimden market.

So every afternoon, she turned on the hot tap above her bath, and enjoyed the clean scent of soap, and the sound of running water, and the swirling mist of steam for half an hour or so.

Because she was so kind, her front door was never locked, for she could not bear to think that any visitor should knock and have no answer.

As usual, the door was ajar when the two scarecrows and the lamb reached it.

Upsidaisy, who was proud of her education, read aloud the notice pinned above the brass knocker: PLEASE WALK IN AND TAP ON BATHROOM DOOR.

'I casn't think how she knew we was comin',' muttered Earthy Mangold.

'The Cruelty Lady knows a lot!'

Upsidaisy pushed against the door, and trundled into the little hall.

'Maybe she was expectin' woodpeckers,' said Earthy, 'they're the best tappers I knows.'

The lamb pranced and skidded on the polished linoleum.

'They dip sheep in baths,' said Earthy suspiciously. 'I'll not let that Cruelty Lady dip Lamb-love – not till the weather's warmer.'

Upsidaisy trundled forward: she had seen another notice on the door opposite. The word BATHROOM was printed on a piece of paper fastened by a drawing-pin to a white panel.

Neither Earthy Mangold's twiggy fingers, nor Upsidaisy's paper-stuffed gloves could tap very well. One scrabbled, the other padded, but there was no reply from inside except the sound of water gushing from the taps.

'Maybe she's drowned hersel',' said Upsidaisy anxiously. 'It sounds there's a river runnin' in there that's louder than Scatterbrook stream in flood.'

The lamb danced forward and butted against the door – once, twice and three times.

'Who is that?' asked a voice, and the sound of rushing water was silenced.

'It's usses,' replied Mangold.

'It's wee's,' corrected Upsidaisy, proud of her grammar.

'Ma-aa! Ma-aa! Ma-aa!' bleated the lamb.

'Has a sheep hurt itself?' shouted Miss Armitage.

'It's Lamb-love,' replied Earthy.

'We wants you to keep it safe,' added Upsidaisy, 'there's dreadful things goin' on in Miss Dollit's gardin'. They've made a statute out o' one lamb – a lamb and a monkey. I've seen pickters o' monkeys, and I knows.'

'Wait a minute. I'll be out as quickly as I can.'

Inside the bathroom Miss Armitage was drying herself on a huge towel. Outside, the lamb was bleating frantically as it leaped on the linoleum which was nearly as slippery as ice.

The bathroom door opened outwards, and the scarecrows were standing by its hinged side. Presently, there was the sound of a key turning in a lock. This was followed by the squeak of hinges. Steam poured out into the hall, and Earthy Mangold and Upsidaisy were nearly flattened between wall and door.

'Where are you?' asked Miss Armitage.

She stood, wrapped in the huge towel, her hair dripping,

her bare legs pink from scrubbing, and peered through the dense steam.

Two voices answered in chorus from behind the door.

'Please to look arter Lamb-love.'

'They've statuted a lamb in Miss Dollit's gardin' – a lamb and a monkey!'

'They're going to statute Thing-love!'

Earthy Mangold, pushed by Upsidaisy, edged out from between door and wall.

The steam had cleared a little by now, and Miss Armitage was just able to see the small figure in the head-scarf and twin-set.

'Are you one of the school children?' she asked.

'*I'm* from the school!' replied Upsidaisy proudly. 'You said to tell if childers was cruel. It's Marlene Snooks done it. The lamb and the monkey's all over conerete set hard like that statute genelman in the school yard.'

'Oh!' exclaimed Miss Armitage, 'surely not? I always thought Marlene Snooks was such a kind little girl.'

'She's bein' not kind today in Miss Dollit's gardin',' replied Upsidaisy from behind the door.

'But I can't imagine any child doing such a wicked thing! Are you quite sure you are not making up stories?'

Miss Armitage remembered the day when Tommy Higginsthwaite, who was rather impertinent, and fond of practical joking, had told her that some boys were robbing a mare's nest in Farmer Braithewaite's meadow.

The lamb, tired of skidding on linoleum, made a little skittering rush past her legs and landed on the bathmat.

'Please to look arter Lamb-love. Please to comfort her!' pleaded Earthy, so softly and sadly that Miss Armitage's kind heart was touched.

'Of course I will,' she said. 'You two children had better wait here until I have put some clothes on. Then you can show me exactly what has happened. I shan't be long.'

The bathroom door slammed behind her and the lamb. The two scarecrows were left standing alone in the hall.

'I hope as she won't sheep-dip Lamb-love,' said Earthy Mangold anxiously.

'Marlene Snooks is more like to come back and statute Mr Gummidge,' replied Upsidaisy. 'I give him warnin' but he fell into a sulk outside the summer-house. He'd be more easy to statute when he's sulkin' nor when he's walkin' about. I give him warnin' but it weren't no use.'

'Oh, Upsidaisy-love!' cried Earthy, 'we casn't wait here no longer. We must save Mr Gummidge afore it's too late. I casn't abear to think o' bein' wife to a statuted husbin!'

Only a passing motorist on his way to London saw the two scarecrows as they tottered and trundled across the road, and he was in far too great a hurry to take much notice.

As they went they chattered wildly.

'If Mr Gummidge won't come out o' his sulk there won't be nothin' for it but to cover him with leaves same as the robins did,' said Upsidaisy.

'Mr Gummidge never has been covered with leaves by robins!' Earthy's voice sounded very shocked. 'He'd not demean himsel'!'

'If you was eddicate same as me, you'd know the story o' the Babes in the Wood,' said Upsidaisy. 'The babes had a wicked uncle as wanted to statute 'em same as Marlene wants to statute Mr Gummidge, so they hid in a wood, and the robins covered 'em all over wi' dry leaves.'

'Beggin' your pardon, and if it's all the same to you, Mr Gummidge wouldn't like that sort o' impullence from robins.' Earthy spoke almost crossly because she was so worried. 'Asides, leaves isn't dry at this time o' year, and Mr Gummidge'd take a lot more coverin' nor two babies would.'

'Then we'll have to pick green leaves from trees, and throw 'em at him,' argued Upsidaisy, 'and, somehows, we'll have to unsulk him and make him lay down so's the leaves don't fall off o' him.'

'We'll see what we'll do when we gets to the summer-house,' said Earthy. 'If they statutes Mr Gummidge they must statute me, so's I'll know how he feels, and stand more chanst o' comfortin' him.'

Suddenly she stood still, and cried, 'Oh! Thing-love!'

She had reached the place where the Teddy Bear, soaked and dark with oil, lolled against the concrete-covered toy lamb.

'Oh, Thing-love!' she repeated, 'come to Earthy! Oh, Lamb-love, you don't look right!'

'There won't be no time to pick leaves to throw at Mr Gummidge if you don't come quick,' said Upsidaisy.

Clutching the Teddy Bear so tightly that the oil oozed from its fur, Earthy followed her friend to the summer-house.

Worzel Gummidge had gone!

'He'll be a statute by now!' remarked Upsidaisy. 'Maybe they've set him up alongside the statuted genelman in the school playground. He'll be more company for me now nor he'll be for you, seein' as you aren't eddicate enough to work in school allotments.'

A sparrow flew by. In its beak it carried a stiff straw from one of Worzel Gummidge's boots. A few more straws were scattered on the path leading to the orchard. Earthy Man-gold followed the trail, and Upsidaisy came after. A fourth straw lay in the gap of a hedge dividing the orchard from a meadow. Beyond the meadow, as Earthy knew, though she could not see it, lay the triangular field that was next to the railway allotments.

'Maybe Mr Gummidge is havin' a chat with Mildew Turmut,' she said. 'Come along o' me, Upsidaisy.'

So it was that by the time Miss Armitage had dressed her-self and had bundled the lamb into her own chicken-run, and had hurried across the road, there was no sign of a scarecrow in the garden of *The Treasure Ship*.

The gnomes were there, so was the monkey, and so was the concrete-covered lamb, so was Miss Dollit, and so was Marlene Snooks.

Miss Dollit looked very pleased indeed. Miss Armitage hurried forward just in time to hear her say. 'What a very clever idea, Marlene! You must have worked hard.'

The little girl, whose hands were full of small tins of paint, mumbled an answer. (She had to mumble because she was holding a paint-brush in her mouth. Two more brushes were stuck behind her ears.)

Miss Armitage was almost too angry to speak. At first she had not quite believed her strange visitors of a quarter-of-an-hour ago. But here, just as they had said, was Marlene Snooks. Here, too, was Miss Dollit whom she had once met at a village jumble sale. There was a toy lamb, looking as large as life in its thick coat of concrete. Beside it was the poor monkey.

Marlene dropped the paint-brush from her mouth, licked some grey undercoating from her lips, and exclaimed, 'It's the Cruelty Lady!'

'How very nice of you to call!' said Miss Dollit, and she held out her hand. 'It's Miss Armitage, I think?'

Miss Armitage looked at the hand in the way that Mrs Marble might have looked at a black beetle. Then she pointed to the lamb –

'Th'at! Th'at!' she stuttered.

'Yes, wasn't it a clever idea!' Miss Dollit answered brightly.

'I did it for a surprise – that and the monkey,' explained Marlene. 'I wanted to paint them, though, before Miss Dollit saw them.'

'Have you anything that will dissolve concrete?' Miss

Armitage dropped to her knees, and began to tug at a curl of concrete clinging to the woollen coat of the lamb. 'Quickly! There's no time to lose! I may be able to loosen some of the stuff with a hammer or something.'

She picked up a stone, and began to tap gently at the concrete round the 'statute's' mouth.

'She's spoiling my lamb!' whined Marlene.

'May I ask why you are behaving in this extraordinary way?' asked Miss Dollit.

Miss Armitage answered jerkily, as she continued to tap, 'I should have thought (*tap*) that would have been clear to anyone (*tap*). Please, go to the Post Office (*tap*) and telephone to the Vet (*tap*). Tell him what has happened and ask him to come as quickly as possible.'

'The Vet?' repeated Miss Dollit, 'why do you want the Vet?'

'So that he can try to save this lamb, though I'm afraid it's too late (*tap*). If the Vet is not in, please telephone to the R.S.P.C.A. at Dimden (*tap*). Please hurry.'

'The R.S.P.C.A.!' repeated Miss Dollit. 'Do you mean the Royal Society for the Prevention of Cruelty to Animals?'

'I said she was the Cruelty Lady!' put in Marlene, 'but I wish she wouldn't spoil my surprise lamb.'

Suddenly Miss Dollit understood, and laughed brightly.

'Surely,' she said, 'surely you can't imagine that Marlene has covered a L I V E lamb with concrete. As though any nice child would do such a wicked thing! Marlene, tell Miss Armitage all about your surprise.'

But Marlene had turned away. She was squatting on the ground beside the monkey, and her brush was flicking in and out of a tin of red paint.

*Silly old thing!* thought Marlene. *Silly old Cruelty Lady to spoil my surprise*. Her pink tongue moved from side to side of her mouth as she worked.

'Marlene!' repeated Miss Dollit sharply, and suddenly she did not feel very sure about anything.

'There WAS a live lamb in the orchard!' she gasped.
'Yes, there was a live lamb.'

'So the two school children told me (*tap*). I have put one lamb into my chicken-run for safety. Now, will you telephone or must I?'

'I will,' said Miss Dollit, as she hurried away.

*Silly old things*, thought Marlene, as a trickle of red paint dripped on to her lap. *Silly, silly, SILLY things. As though I'd dip a live lamb in concrete!*

Miss Armitage was working hard on the lamb, and several tufts of rather scruffy wool showed between the concrete curls.

*She'll look silly when the Vet comes*, thought Marlene. *Serve her right for thinking I'd hurt a lamb. Let her find out for herself. Why should I tell her? It'll be fun when she finds out.*

She was (and, really there is no wonder) feeling hurt over the behaviour of the 'Cruelty Lady' and of Miss Dollit. She was angry with Robin, and disappointed because she had not been able to finish her surprise. These three things made her feel savage.

*It'll be lots of fun!* she thought miserably. *I'll laugh a lot.*

But poor Marlene was not to laugh just yet!

Mrs Briggs, who was the best washerwoman in Scatterbrook, and whose face looked so clean that it might have been carved from the best white soap, marched into the garden. She was dragging a very small, very curly-headed boy by the hand, and she was carrying a paper sunshade. At least, the object she clutched in her left hand *had* been a sunshade once upon time. Now a few tatters of black and orange paper flapped from its bent ribs. The yellow tassel that dangled from its handle had only a few shreds left. The sunshade was neither pretty nor useful.

'So there you are, Marlene Snooks! Gloria from the Post Office saw you coming here with Ron's baa-lamb. I met her at the bus stop,' said Mrs Briggs.

She jerked at the little boy's hand, and lowered her voice.

'Speak up for yourself, Ron. Ask Marlene what's she done with the pretty baa-lamb your Dad gave you for Christmas.'

'She took it!' whimpered Ronald.

'Stole it, you mean,' prompted Mrs Briggs.

'I didn't, then!' said Marlene. She stood up, and the little pool of paint from her lap trickled in crimson runnels down her skirt. 'I didn't, then! He wanted the sunshade. He liked the way it opened up and shut down. He liked the way the clicker worked. He liked it more than the lamb.'

'Liked the clicker!' agreed Ronald, swinging himself forward and grabbing at the sunshade. 'LIKE the clicker!'

'Well I never!' said Mrs Briggs. 'Did you ever! He was crying like a wet washing-day when I found him in the garden after I'd brought in the towels from the line. He said he was crying for his baa-lamb.'

'He can have it, then!' shouted Marlene. 'It's all spoiled now.'

She waved her paint-brush in the direction of the lamb, and Mrs Briggs darted forward. Below the chunky legs of the lamb and from among a scattering of concrete, a bit of green painted board showed clearly.

'I'd know that toy baa-lamb anywhere!' declared Mrs Briggs.

She put her hands underneath the lamb, and tugged hard. Because she was so much stronger than Marlene, because her hands, so used to wringing heavy sheets and towels, had a firmer grip, the board left the concrete quite easily, and only splintered a little.

Miss Armitage, who had been looking more and more confused, dropped her stone, and exclaimed. 'But it's a *toy* lamb!'

'It was till you started spoiling it!' said Mrs Briggs sourly. 'A nice sort of toy it is now! Ron would cut his precious head on that nasty hard stuff a dozen times a day if he started playing with it. It beats me why you wanted to smother it in concrete.'

'I was trying to uncover it,' explained poor Miss Armitage, holding out a tuft of dingy wool attached to a curl of concrete.

'That lamb came up white as snow after a good wash in soapy water. Ron will cry himself to sleep tonight I shouldn't wonder.' Mrs Briggs turned to the little boy, 'You'll cry yourself to sleep tonight, won't you, my precious?'

But Ronald, smiling happily, was twirling the sunshade round and round above his head.

Miss Dollit, breathless from running, hurried into the garden. 'The Post Office is shut!' she gasped, 'I forgot it was early closing day. I shall have to use Mrs Bloomsbury-Barton's telephone.'

Marlene wiped the red-bristled paint-brush on the grass. So she was not going to have any fun after all. She tip-toed away, leaving the grown-up people to argue, while Ronald played with his sunshade.

Soon, they too, left the garden – Miss Armitage to feed the lamb, Miss Dollit to search the orchard for Upsidaisy, and Ronald to play with the Japanese sunshade. Mrs Briggs had been given money enough to buy a bigger and a better toy. Only a concrete-covered lamb and a paint-streaked monkey remained as memorials to a very peculiar day.

# 7 Saucy Nancy

*The Treasure Ship* was very nearly ready for the spring visitors. Several enormous orange umbrellas were dotted about in the garden. Underneath them chairs and green tables were set out in readiness for tea. A few stone rabbits kept company with the gnomes, the monkey and the concrete lamb, and the toadstools.

Inside the largest room of *The Treasure Ship* itself there were other tables covered with antiques – pieces of old china, small china figures and cottages, horse-brasses, snuff-boxes, silver candlesticks, brass candlesticks, bronze candlesticks, ships-in-bottles, glass rolling-pins, and many other treasures.

Marlene, forgiven now for the affair of the concrete lamb, had spent hours in dusting, polishing, sorting, mending and arranging. She and Miss Dollit were glad that the Easter holidays had begun.

On a special table in a special corner of the room were the special things that Miss Dollit had made herself. There were pen-wipers, shaped like chickens, and needle-books in the shapes of cottages, and nightdress cases in the shapes of cats and dogs. There were pencils with little crochet-hats glued to their tops. Miss Dollit had collected shells and stuck them together and painted them until they had lost their shining beauty and looked like strange and ugly birds and insects.

Old Mrs Dollit, who had come to share *The Treasure Ship* with her daughter, shuddered whenever she passed the special table, for she was as downright and as sensible as Miss Dollit was skittish.

She was standing by the table on this particular rainy morning, and she was looking disgustedly at a row of yellow felt egg-cosies that were shaped like the heads of chickens.

'I can't think why you do it, Phoebe.'

'Do what, Mother?'

'Bother to cut felt about, and embroider eyes and beaks on it!'

'But the egg-cosies are such FUN, Mother!'

'I shouldn't have thought it would have amused an egg to be reminded of what it might have been if it hadn't been boiled.'

Miss Dollit giggled, and her mother picked up a plush rabbit dressed in a wide quilted skirt with a muslin apron.

'Now I do call that a waste of good stuff. It would have made the dearest little matinée coat for a baby.'

'But, Mother dear, that's a nightdress case. The rabbit will lie on top of the bedspread with the nightie tucked away under its skirt.'

Mrs Dollit snorted.

'Rabbits are all right. Nightdress cases are all right, I suppose, for people who like them. But what *is* the sense of keeping a night-gown *in* a rabbit *in* a skirt and apron?'

'Just for fun!' said poor Miss Dollit.

Mrs Dollit picked up a big pencil from a tray. The pencil's top was decorated with a blob of gold sealing wax from which dangled a long silk tassel.

'I shouldn't like to have the back of *my* hand tickled all the time I was writing,' she said, and went to the window.

Worzel Gummidge, who had been brought back by Miss Dollit from the railway allotment where he had been spending a few days with his sister, Mildew Turmut, was standing by the little pool. His broomstick legs were planted in the painted drain-pipe. One arm dropped beneath the

weight of a macintosh. His turnip face was sad and sulky;
and raindrops trickled from the brim of his old hat.

'You'd better have that scarecrow moved tomorrow,' said
Mrs Dollit. 'The sight of it will put people off their teas.
Luckily it's too wet for anyone to turn up today.'

'But I put him there on purpose!' exclaimed Miss Dollit,
'I put him there so that people can use him as a hat-and-
coat-stand. I'm sure they'll love Old Man Scarecrow. He's
such fun!'

'Oh, well,' Mrs Dollit sniffed again, 'oh, well, I suppose
you must do as you think best. If you want the tea-garden
to look like a field, why don't you buy a hay rick and a farm
cart, and put a lot of mud on the grass? If you want it to be
a rabbit warren, why don't you buy some live rabbits instead of those stone things?'

While Mrs Dollit was wishing that her daughter would
not waste her time in making crochet hats for pencils, and
Miss Dollit was longing for her mother to understand that a
scarecrow is a most suitable inhabitant of a tea-garden, the
ship's bell outside the front door of *The Treasure Ship* rang
loudly.

'I wonder you don't have a fog-horn as well!' muttered
Mrs Dollit sourly as her daughter hurried to open the door.

The Rowstock brothers had brought an immense packing-case from the station. Miss Dollit asked them to carry
it to the garage which was used as a store-room.

'And could you unpack it for me, please?' she said. 'I
have to go now.'

The Rowstock brothers looked doubtful, and the elder
one explained that they must go back to the station at once
to collect a load of coal.

'I daresay the nipper could do it for you,' said the younger
brother, jerking a thumb towards Robin, who had been
enjoying a free ride on the coal cart.

'Of course!' cried Miss Dollit. 'Boys are so good with

nails and things. Be careful, Robin, won't you? I'll help you as soon as I get back from the White House. And, Robin, while you are in the garage, will you see if Polly needs some fresh drinking water? Do see if you can make her talk.'

Polly was a grey parrot with a pink tail, and it was a great disappointment to Miss Dollit because though it screeched very loudly, it would say nothing but 'Poor Polly! Pretty Polly!'

She had bought it from Mrs Kibbins's sailor nephew, and the man had declared it was a grand talker.

'It's shy with strangers,' he had said. 'You keep it in a room by itself for a bit till it starts talking to itself for company. Then you'll be surprised.'

That is why the parrot's cage was kept in the garage, but, so far, the bird had not surprised anyone.

'What's in that great packing-case?' asked Mrs Dollit when her daughter had come back into the room.

'It's a surprise, Mother – a lovely surprise, but I'll tell YOU. You remember my friend, Virginia, who lives at Seashell?'

'The one who wears sandals, and frocks that look like sacks?'

'Yes. Virginia's SO original, and so clever at buying antiques. She wrote to say she had found an old ship's figurehead in a shipyard, and had sent it to me as a birthday present!'

'What can you do with it?' demanded Mrs Dollit.

'I shall put her up in the tea-garden. She hasn't got any legs, of course, so I shall have to prop her up in a tree or somewhere. She's got an outstretched arm —'

'A figurehead in a tea-garden!' repeated Mrs Dollit, 'a figurehead in a tea-garden! People will think you've lost your reason, Phoebe!'

'But you don't understand! A Treasure Ship and a figurehead GO together. I thought of putting a tray into her out-stretched hand. I shall make paper boats from paper table-napkins, and the visitors can help themselves.'

'I should have live lobsters crawling round while you're about it!' said Mrs Dollit. 'I'm going to finish my knitting upstairs.'

When her mother had gone, Miss Dollit hurried off to the White House.

In the meantime Robin was hunting for a hammer and screwdriver among the junk in the garage.

The packing-case was made of slats, and there were wide gaps between them. Through one gap, much wider than the others, a painted wooden hand and an arm extended.

*It must be another scarecrow*, thought Robin, *but it's got an arm like a woman's, and it smells like the fish fertilizer in that field of Farmer Braithewaite's. No it doesn't – not quite – it smells fresh sort-of.*

He stumbled against the packing-case, and the unforget-table salty tang of deep-sea breezes and tar and paint and oil and freshness whiffed out at him.

Robin had never been to sea – only to the seaside, and that only once – but he had not forgotten that particular mixture of smells. It excited him, and he sniffed again. It excited the parrot into sea-speech.

'Shiver my timbers!' screeched the bird.

*Wish I could find that old screwdriver and hammer quickly*, thought Robin.

As though he had spoken his thoughts aloud, a voice from inside the crate replied, 'Look at my finger, landlubber! See where it's pointing.'

The forefinger of the painted hand was pointing to a jumble of old fire-irons under the table on which stood the parrot's cage.

Robin picked up a bent poker that did its job as well as

any screwdriver or crowbar. He wiggled the point of it under a slat, and then pushed downwards.

'Heave-ho, me hearty!'

The words were spoken by a rusty voice from inside the crate, and then, as Robin wrestled with the slats, the voice broke into song –

> 'I thought I heard the North Sea call,
>     Calling Saucy Nancy,
>   But here there is no salt at all
>     Nor anything I fancy.'

'I shan't be a sec!' gasped Robin, as a couple of shining nails creaked from their holes, and the smell of pinewood sawdust mingled with the other scents.

The singing grew louder –

> 'I thought I heard the South Seas stir
>     From sleep, to sigh for Nancy –
>   "Has nobody the news of her?
>     For she's the one we fancy."
>
> 'She's due to sail the seas again,
>     According to her fancy
>   While stars above a sea-salt lane
>     Shine down on Saucy Nancy.'

With a groan and a creak the last slat of the lid came up, and Robin was tugging at the sacks that covered the figure in the crate. She lay on her side. A ragged fishing-net shawl was draped round her shoulders. Her painted cheek was as red as though it had been newly lashed by spray.

'Haul me up, young shaver!' she shouted in a rusty voice. 'Heave-ho, me hearty!'

Robin seized her by the shoulders and tugged, but before he could free her arm, he had to knock away the slats from the side of the crate. While he was working the figurehead talked in a language that was as strange as French to him.

'Roll me in bilge-water! Pickle me in grog! Look slippy, you spit-to-wind'ard son of a limpet!'

'Heave-ho! Up she rises!' screeched the parrot as the figurehead's shoulders rose above the edge of the crate, and rested against it. She had only one arm, and that stretched straight out ahead of her. She had no legs but a tangle of fishing-net tied to her waist made a sort of skirt.

Her painted face was rather beautiful though it was chipped and cracked in places. Her carved hair was black and shining; it lay in a coil on the back of her neck. Her eyes were bright blue, as Robin saw when he stood in front of her.

'Who are you?' she asked, and her finger pointed straight towards him.

'I'm Robin.'

'There was a cabin boy called Robin sailed with us on the China Run. He spent all his spare time in the crow's nest, looking for a sight of land. Never knew anyone so landsick.'

'He must've been small to get inside a crow's nest,' said Robin.

The figurehead laughed hoarsely.

'It wasn't a nest made by birds,' she said. 'I've seen your inland crows. You see more ravens and jackdaws flying out o' the cliffs when we get near land.'

'Are you a sea-scarecrow?' asked Robin.

'Scarecrow!' she repeated. 'I'm a figurehead! Me name's Saucy Nancy, landlubber, and you remember that.'

'Yes,' said Robin politely.

'Say "Aye! Aye!" when you speak to me or I'll have you rolled in the scuppers! What's this place?'

'It's called *The Treasure Ship.*'

'Ship? It's no more like a ship than a lobster is. There's something that belongs to a ship though.'

Saucy Nancy swung her arm until her outstretched finger

was pointing to a blue glass rolling-pin on a packing case. 'Give it to me, young shaver.'

Robin picked up the rolling-pin and, as he held it out, the figurehead's fingers curved round the shining surface, and she bent her elbow.

'They used to smuggle grog in those,' she muttered. 'I'm parched for want of a tot of grog!'

The cork at the end of the rolling-pin did not fit properly, and in another second a shower of coloured bath-salts descended on Saucy Nancy's shawl, and lay there like spangles.

The parrot laughed raucously as the figurehead flung the rolling-pin across the garage.

'What's that stuff?' she asked. 'It looks like fish scales but it smells worse than a cargo of lubberly roots. What is it?'

'Coffee sugar,' replied Robin. 'The big grocer in Dimden sells it.'

He scooped up a handful of the coloured crystals, popped them into his mouth and then spat them out disgustedly.

'It's b-bath-salts!' he spluttered.

Of course Robin did not use bath-salts. He scrubbed himself with good carbolic soap which smelled a little like Nancy's fishing-net shawl. Once, though, when he was staying with his Aunt Emily, she had (for a 'treat' which was no treat) tipped some bath-salts into his washing-water. That was why he recognized the scent.

'Bath-salts!' repeated Saucy Nancy. 'There's enough salt in the sea-bath, isn't there? Bath-salts in a smuggler's rolling-pin! Fetch me some grog, young shaver. The reek of that stuff makes me sicker than bilge-water makes a home-sick cabin boy.'

'Splice the mainbrace!' shouted the parrot. 'Pretty Polly!'

'That's a seafarin' bird if ever there was one,' said Saucy Nancy approvingly.

'How do *you* know?' asked Robin.

*He* knew, of course, because he had been present when

the sailor sold the parrot to Miss Dollit.

'By the cut of its jib, that's how I know. See how it climbs the riggin!'

Claw over grey claw, the parrot was mounting to the top of its cage.

'Splice the mainbrace!' it wheezed.

'Give it a tot of grog, landlubber!' demanded Saucy Nancy.

Words from a book (*Treasure Island*) that his father had read aloud came back to Robin's mind –

> 'Fifteen men on a dead man's chest
> Ro-to-to and a bottle of rum!
> Drink and the devil had done the rest –
> Ro-to-to and a bottle of rum.'

He remembered having been told that grog was the same as rum. He remembered now that his father had explained that rum was a sweet drink. He fumbled in his pocket, and felt the comforting chink of coppers.

'I could get a bottle of lemonade from the Post Office,' he said obligingly.

Nancy flung her arm ceilingwards. 'Roll me in bilgewater! Pickle me in grog! Lemonade for a seafarin' parrot! What have I come to? The shipyard was bad enough. Then I was salvaged by a spit-to-wind'ard, beach-combing SHE that looked like a bundle o' mothers' washing hung in the shrouds. Then I was crated, then I was run on wheels, then I was brought here to listen to lemonade-talk!'

'Sorry!' muttered Robin, and he did feel sorry for the poor figurehead.

A shaft of sunlight streaming through the window shone on the crack below her left eye, and the crack sparkled as though it were filled with crusted salt.

*She's crying*, thought Robin. *She's brave all right, but she's crying.*

He turned his head away so that the figurehead should not see that he had noticed the crustiness.

Perhaps Saucy Nancy understood his feelings because she spoke more gently –

'You cut and run, young shaver. You've got the legs, and I've not. Go and find your sea-legs.'

'Do you mean RUN-AWAY-TO SEA?' asked Robin.

Suddenly (perhaps because the garage had become filled by sea-magic) he felt that nothing could be grander. He could go now, just as he was. There was nothing in the world to stop him. Beyond the land there was the sea which he had only seen for once on a still summer's day. He could be a stowaway and sail and climb rigging. His thoughts were muddled memories of stories in books but they were very grand indeed.

'Run-away-to sea!' repeated Robin.

'Where else would a boy run?' asked Nancy. 'Take me with you out of this lubberly hole. You and me and the parrot will have fine times at sea.'

But the figurehead was heavy, and Robin did not quite trust the parrot who had tweaked his ear rather badly the day before.

'You can be cabin boy and work your way up,' continued Saucy Nancy. 'The parrot can live in the galley, and I'll go back to my old job.'

'What job?' asked Robin.

'Guiding the ship, of course, pointing the way across the water. That's been my job —'

Raising her rusty voice, the figurehead sang –

> 'Yes, I shall go a-sailing,
>    Since sailing is my pleasure –
> I'm set to go a-sailing,
>    And you'll come, too.'

Robin recognized the tune of *We'll go no more a-roving*, and the parrot screeched excitedly, while Nancy continued –

> 'We both shall go a-sailing
> Across the windy waters,
> And seek the mermaids' daughters
> And the dolphins' sons.'

The door opened, and Miss Dollit bounced into the garage.

'Why, Robin!' she said, 'why, Robin, I didn't know you could sing. And you've unpacked the figurehead. Isn't she a beauty?'

'Splice the mainbrace!' yelled the parrot. 'Roll me in bilge-water! Tap out the weevils! Three sheets in the wind! Pretty Polly!'

'And you've taught Polly to talk!' cried Miss Dollit delightedly. 'I knew it could.'

The parrot blinked a grey eye, raised a grey claw and scratched its grey head.

'Scratch a Poll!' it muttered. 'Pretty Polly! Pretty Polly! Pretty Polly!'

'Say what you said before, that's a good bird!' begged Miss Dollit, but the parrot continued its monotonous muttering, 'Pretty Polly! Pretty Polly! Pretty Polly!'

'Perhaps it's shy of M E,' said Miss Dollit.

'Spit to wind'ard daughter of a limpet!' yelled Saucy Nancy, and her voice was so like the parrot's that Robin could not be absolutely certain which of them had spoken, though he was almost sure.

'Misery in the crow's nest! Bilge-dripping sea-slug!'

'Robin!' exclaimed Miss Dollit, 'surely Y O U didn't teach the bird to say that?'

Robin shook his head.

'I hoped not. I'm afraid Mrs Kibbins's nephew can't have

been a very polite man. Never mind, we must teach it some jolly things that will amuse the visitors. Then its cage can hang in the tree beside Saucy Nancy.'

The timber from which Saucy Nancy was carved really shivered then, but luckily Miss Dollit was not looking at her. Only Robin noticed the crusty tear that glistened under the figurehead's left eye, and saw the bath-salts falling from mesh to mesh of the fishing-net shawl. Only *he* heard the deep sigh, and sniffed the salty breath that drifted across the garage.

'Yes,' continued Miss Dollit, 'we must teach it some jolly expressions like *Ship Ahoy* and *Jolly Jack Tar* and *Rule Britannia*.'

'Pretty Polly!' murmured the parrot sulkily.

Miss Dollit was thinking of another plan, and now she spoke of it.

'I might be able to buy some sailor suits for you and Marlene – bell-bottom trousers for you, and a pleated skirt for her. You could help to serve the teas on busy days – only during the holidays, of course. I could teach you to dance the horn-pipe. Wouldn't that be fun?'

Again, a breath of sea breeze drifted across the garage, as Saucy Nancy sighed.

Robin did not answer. He was afraid that Marlene might like a sailor suit but he had seen pictures of them. He did not want to share his new friend with anyone in the world.

'Weevils and barnacles!' sighed Saucy Nancy.

# 8 Pretty Polly

After all, Saucy Nancy was not set up to shiver her timbers in the younger timbers of an apple-tree because Miss Dollit had been given a wonderful present by the village builder. The present was a sundial, rather worn and chipped, but, as she said, it would make a perfect pedestal for the parrot's cage, or for the figurehead.

In the end, she had decided that the cage could hang from the apple-tree in fine weather, and that the figurehead on the sundial could stand just below with a cluster of stone rabbits at her feet.

So there, her fishing-net skirt sweeping to the grass, and covering the sundial's stem, was Saucy Nancy. Her out-stretched arm pointed towards *The Treasure Ship* as though in mockery.

Robin found her there on the morning after the meeting in the garage. It was just after breakfast. Already Miss Dollit had hung the parrot's cage in the tree. Mrs Dollit was making cakes to be served with the mid-morning coffee. Worzel Gummidge, still standing in the painted drain-pipe, sulked by the summer-house. Earthy Mangold, back in the orchard with her lamb, was talking to a beetle. Everything was very peaceful.

As Robin took the short cut through the orchard, Earthy Mangold interrupted her talk to the beetle, and looked up.

'Do please to ask Mr Gummidge to give over bein' a hat-stand,' she pleaded. 'I've more nor what I can do with lookin' arter Lamb-love and Thing-love, and Beetle-love.'

The Teddy Bear, still oil sodden, lay on the grass beside her. Mary, the lamb, was playing *King of the Castle* on a tree-stump and the beetle was scuttling away.

'All right,' said Robin, 'all right, but I want to see a friend first.'

Even the sight of the Teddy Bear with its oil-soaked tummy did not touch his heart now. He wanted to find Saucy Nancy, and to hear more of her wild sea talk.

'I've comforted Thing-love the best ways I could,' said Earthy, 'I've rubbed him all over me smart skirt.'

(Indeed, her skirt was sadly oil-streaked.)

'Lamb-love's licked Thing-love, but he don't seem to fancy the taste.'

(Indeed, the lamb's soft nose was dark with oil.)

'I never thought to be wife to a hat-stand.'

'ALL RIGHT.'

Robin's voice was impatient, but he could not help that. All night he had been dreaming about ships and running-away-to-sea. All through his dreams he had heard Saucy Nancy's singing.

'Maybe I'd best come along and talk to Mr Gummidge mesel',' said Earthy, and she stumbled after Robin. 'You help me talk to him, beggin' your pardon, and if it's all the same to you. Gimme your hand while we walks along.'

Of course Robin, because he was very kind-hearted, really, could not resist the clutch of Earthy's twiggy fingers. All the same, because of his hurry, he pulled a little.

'Oh, Worzel, love,' said Earthy, when Robin first, and she three seconds later, had reached the summer-house, 'do please to give over bein' a hat-stand. You casn't LIKE bein' a hat-stand.'

Worzel Gummidge opened one eye, and answered obstinately, 'If I knowed what hat-stands liked I'd know if I liked bein' a hat-stand.'

'I wish you wasn't so argumentative,' said Earthy.

'Maybe hat-stands IS argumentative.'

Gummidge opened his other eye.

'Don't let's quarrel, Worzel, love,' begged Earthy.

'I don't know as hat-stands *does* quarrel. Stands to reason, I don't. Anyways, what one calls a quarrel tother doesn't. If you was to quarrel with a beetle —'

'As though I ever would!' interrupted Earthy.

'I seen you kick one!'

Green tears trickled down Earthy's cheeks.

'Oncst,' she sobbed, 'oncst I pushed a beetle with a loose bottle-straw. The straw come loose and I'd forgot how long me boot was. I right-side-up the beetle and I comforted it all night. I'd never push a beetle on purpose.'

'Purpose don't matter to a kicked beetle!' argued Gummidge. 'If you got kicked by a beetle you'd call it a quarrel!'

'Beggin' your pardon, Worzel, beggin' your pardon and if it's all the same to you, I'd NOT call it a quarrel – not if it was never so.'

Earthy spoke almost indignantly, and Robin murmured, 'My Mum says it takes two to make a quarrel.'

'Ooh aye!' agreed Gummidge, 'stands to reason it takes two to kick a beetle. It takes a beetle and the one that kicks it.'

Green tears rained down Earthy's cheeks as she remembered the beetle that had been pushed so gently by her stray boot-straw. Had that beetle ever been quite such a happy beetle – even after a long night's comforting?

Robin hated tears – wet tears (Saucy Nancy's tears were *different* – dry, with a salty sparkle). He was in a hurry, and tears took time.

'I've got to go now,' he said, and ran down the path.

The parrot, looking rather huffed, was clambering up and down the bars of its cage. Saucy Nancy, her arm quivering with rage or sorrow, was pointed towards *The Treasure Ship*. Dew shinier than fish scales glinted on the meshes of her fishing-net shawl and skirt.

'Is that you, young shaver?' she asked.

'Aye, aye, Miss!' said Robin.

'We didn't have "Misses" in sailin' ships – not when I was in the bows. THEN we might have the skipper's Missus, and she was a tartar. All skippers' missuses was tartars, nosin' about in the galleys, fussin' about the weevils in the hard tack. Weevils was meat to sailors when I was a lass afore I was seasoned.'

'What,' asked Robin, 'what are weevils, please, Missus?'

'That's better!' Saucy Nancy's stiff lips curved into something that was almost like a smile before she answered. 'I'm Missus, and don't you forget it, shaver. Weevils got tapped out o' hard tack (that's ship biscuits) and weevils was meat.'

'Pretty Polly!' announced the parrot, and flung a sunflower seed from between the bars of its cage.

The bird, after its first excitement over meeting Saucy Nancy, and after one night in *The Treasure Ship* with Miss Dollit, was using land-language again.

'Hearts of oak!' said the parrot moodily and rather miserably.

Miss Dollit had repeated the three words to it, over and over and over again, while it had sulked on its perch. Now, its thick grey tongue stirred inside its grey curved beak.

'Hearts of oak!' repeated the parrot. 'Jolly Jack Tar!'

'Hark at it!' yelled Saucy Nancy.

The voice of a figurehead whose voice had, once upon a time, roused echoes from cliffs when her ship was nearing a home-port, startled a chaffinch from an apple-twig.

'Hark at it! What sort o' talk's that from a sea-faring bird? It's no more right command o' sea-faring language than a mermaid. I can see that parrot with a hair-brush in its claw sitting on a rock like an inshore mermaid. The

offshore mermaids haven't any rocks to loll on. They talk
sense, and they talk seaman-like, same as this one don't.'

'Pretty Polly!' said the parrot. 'Scratch a Poll.'

'I'll scratch you with a marline-spike,' shouted Nancy,
'that's what I'll do to you if you don't stop talking that
fancy-Pretty-Polly-kiss-me-talk. I sailed with a parrot that
was something like a parrot. Did you hear that yarn?'

The parrot huddled itself into a silent huff on its perch.

'Did you hear that yarn?' repeated Saucy Nancy.

'D'you mean me?' asked Robin, and added, 'D'you
mean me, Missus?'

The figurehead began her story –

'That was something like a parrot – that bird was. The
skipper was her owner, and he'd learned her to give orders
the same way he did. And the parrot talked like he did.
Well —'

Robin slid down to the grass, and sat there cross-legged
– a hand on each knee.

'Well, the skipper was friends with the first mate, and
they reckoned they'd like to spend a bit o' shore leave together. That was against the regulations. When the skipper
goes ashore, the first mate's left in charge o' the ship so's
to maintain discipline, see?'

'Yes,' said Robin, 'I mean, aye, aye, Missus.'

'Well, the skipper that had the sea-talking parrot
reckoned he could get round the regulations. So he rigged
up his coat and cap with stuffing same as they rigs inland
scarecrows. Then he leaves it in his cabin with the parrot
alongside, and he and the mate slips overboard, leavin' the
parrot to maintain the discipline o' the ship.'

'How could it?' asked Robin.

'It kept on talking like the Captain so the crew thought
it was him in the cabin, talking raging furious sort of talk –
none o' your pier-head stuff – he was a raging furious sort
of man. Nobody dursent stop working when they thought

the skipper might come raging out of his cabin. It would all have gone right if the parrot hadn't taken a fit to leave the cabin. It flew to the bridge and shouted to the men to weigh anchor, *which* they did. Then it shouted to the helmsman who'd been having a nap by the wheel. Next thing we knew we'd put out to sea, and I was humiliated.'

'Why?' asked Robin.

Saucy Nancy sighed gustily and answered, 'I was sea-sick the first time in my life. It wasn't the up and down did it. It was the round and round and round and round. The parrot kept on shouting "Hard a port!" and the helmsman kept on obeying orders and we kept on going round and round and round like a giddy starfish till the skipper swam from shore and boarded us. He'd a job to do it from the water – it was like climbing on to a giddy merry-go-round. Soon as he was on the bridge, he started yelling like a madman. The parrot started contradictin' until the skipper took the wheel. I've never seen a man so furious. Well, it's natural he didn't like to see his ship commanded by a parrot that hadn't learned to change its mind from port to starboard. The parrot was angry too. The things it SAID —'

'What did it say?' asked Robin.

'Pretty Polly!' screeched the parrot abruptly, and Saucy Nancy glared at it.

'The skipper's bird didn't say nothing like *that*. It flew down from the rigging, and walked about the bridge, and screeched at the skipper, "You go back to your funny cage or I'll wring your funny neck, and put a cloth over you!'

'And what happened?' asked Robin.

'Same as what the parrot said would happen!' Saucy Nancy spoke very slowly and solemnly. 'It turned mutinous and wrung the skipper's neck. Then it put him in a cage, and put a cloth over him same as though he'd been a canary.'

'But —' said Robin, after a long pause, 'but —' Then he laughed.

'Aye!' said Nancy, 'if you listen to sea-yarns, young shaver, you've got to sort out what's yarn and what's spin-drift.'

'Wring your funny neck!' screeched the parrot.

'Roll me in bilge-water! Scrub me with holystone! Baste me barnacles, but this bird's going to learn proper sea-talk – not the inshore stuff – before we go to sea together,' said Nancy. 'I'll learn it to speak my mind as well as its own.'

Robin was not sure that Miss Dollit or the visitors would approve, but he made up his mind to learn sea-talk, too.

Miss Dollit, tripping out into the garden, changed his luck. She was followed by Marlene, and she did not look quite so gay as usual.

The truth was that the tea-garden had, so far, been rather a disappointment.

Only a few strangers had visited Scatterbrook since the orange umbrellas had been put up in the garden, and only two of these had stopped for tea. The larder was full of stale buns that had been baked so hopefully by Mrs Dollit.

In vain, the kettles sang on the hob. In vain, Miss Dollit had shown the tea-garden to motorists who had stopped to buy antiques in the shop.

'Perhaps the strangers are shy.' Miss Dollit had said to her mother. 'Perhaps if one or two people were to sit under the umbrellas, other people would join them. You could take your knitting into the garden, Mother, and I could keep on bringing you cups of tea.'

Mrs Dollit had replied that she did not fancy the scare-crows or the gnomes or the rabbits, or the draughts that would cool her tea or the flies that would bathe in it. Her words had put a new idea into Miss Dollit's head.

'Robin!' she called, 'Robin, come here.'

The boy got up from the grass, and hurried away from Saucy Nancy. He wanted to keep her sea-talk a secret from Marlene.

'Robin, do you think your father would lend me an old hat and, perhaps, a macintosh – nothing very good, of course, but something nice and tidy.'

'Dunno!' said Robin.

'Well, you could ask him, couldn't you? I want to dress up Old Man Scarecrow and sit him up at one of the tables so that he will look like a visitor enjoying his tea. We're going to put Old Lady Scarecrow beside him, aren't we, Marlene?'

The little girl nodded. Then she whispered to Robin, and pointed towards Saucy Nancy – 'What's that other ugly old scarecrow doing over there?'

'She's not!' said Robin, meaning that the figurehead was neither a scarecrow nor ugly. He thought she was beautiful, and, in her own way, Nancy *was*.

'She could sit and be enjoying tea, too,' said Marlene. 'I've an old hat Mrs Kibbins threw away – it's trimmed with pansies.'

'I don't think a figurehead would look quite natural at a tea-table,' said Miss Dollit, and the words made Robin feel very fond of her, so fond that he said, 'I'll go and ask Dad if he'll lend us a mac and a hat.'

'A pair of gloves would be useful, too,' said Miss Dollit. 'Tell your father we'll take the greatest care of them.'

On his way through the orchard, Robin picked up the Teddy Bear. He could put it in the woodshed until he had time to clean it. When he reached Finch Cottage, he saw a note tucked under the door-knocker: ONE BIG BROWN AND ONE SMALL WHITE, PLEASE. That meant that his parents were out, and would not be back until after the baker had called. Probably his mother had taken Mary Lou to the shop.

*I might as well clean the Teddy now,* thought Robin, *then it'll be all ready for Mary Lou to remember me by while I'm away at sea. I'll bring her back a parrot, and I'll bring a silk shawl from*

*China for Mum, and a barrel of rum for Dad.*

He soused the bear's coat in turpentine and, as he rubbed, he went on with his sea-thoughts – *They'll be old when I get home. Mary Lou will be as old as Marlene, and I'll have a beard.*

He rubbed his smooth chin with an oily finger.

*I wonder how I'll like eating weevils. I wonder what they look like and if they taste good. I wonder if Mum's left my elevenses in the pantry. I'll go and see. I might as well let the turps soak in and dry off.*

He left the bear on the chopping-block, and ran into the house. Yes, his mother had left an apple pasty on a plate. There was no doubt it was for him because his name – Robin – was spelled in currants on the top.

The taste of the oil and turpentine from his fingers mingled rather oddly with the spiciness of the apples, but the taste reminded him a little of the sea-scent of Saucy Nancy. He turned the taste over and over on his tongue as he meandered back across the orchard. He had forgotten all about the hat and the coat and the gloves, but the sight of Worzel Gummidge and Earthy sitting under a big orange umbrella reminded him.

Miss Dollit, tired of waiting, had hailed Captain Conway as he motored past *The Treasure Ship.* It was his habit to throw caps and coats and gloves into the back of his car because he was not a very tidy man. This was just as well, for a tidier one might not have cared to lend his clothes to a scarecrow.

So there sat Worzel Gummidge with a check cap tilted rakishly over his turnip-top sprouting hair. There was a yellow muffler round his neck. He was wearing wash-leather gloves and a raincoat.

There was no change in Earthy's clothes except that her twiggy fingers had been pushed into a pair of red woollen gloves belonging to Mrs Conway. A plaid rug was spread over the scarecrows' legs, hiding Gummidge's bottle-straw boots and Earthy's flapping stocking.

Really, the two looked almost as human as humans. Their table was quite a long way away from Saucy Nancy's sundial.

Earthy smiled happily at Robin.

'We're visitors now,' she announced, 'we're visitors enjoyin' our teas, and Mr Gummidge has left off of bein' a hat-stand.'

Worzel Gummidge did not look as though he were enjoying anything very much. He was staring moodily at his wash-leather gloves.

'It's a good thing as humans hasn't more nor five fingers,' he muttered, 'else the rest'd be left outside o' these finger-covers.'

'I've more nor five fingers,' boasted Earthy. 'There's six on one hand and seven on tother, not countin' the ones that snapped off.'

'Stands to reason it's a good thing as centipedes isn't human,' continued Gummidge. 'If they was human they'd want a lot of trousy legs.'

'They'd look sweet in trousy legs,' said Earthy, 'but it'd be sad not havin' hands to put in all their pockets.'

'What'd they keep in their pockets asides the hands they've not got?'

'Hankerchers,' said Earthy, 'lots and lots o' little hankerchers.'

'Hankerchers!' snorted Gummidge. 'Don't talk so daft! If centipedes without hands started usin' hankerchers they'd have to twist their noses back a long way to reach their hankerchers. How'd a long centipede reach the furtherst pocket?'

A little bell was lying on the table beside him. Fumblingly, the scarecrow clutched the brass handle, and rang the bell furiously.

Robin wondered what would happen next. He knew the bell had been put there so that visitors could ring when they wanted tea or coffee.

The back door of *The Treasure Ship* opened, and Mrs Dollit came out. She walked rather carefully because she had mislaid her spectacles.

'Good morning,' she said when she reached the scarecrows. 'Would you like tea or coffee?'

'We've been told to be visitors enjoyin' our teas,' replied Earthy.

'Certainly. Would you like Indian or China?'

'I'd a friend oncst as swallered some china,' answered Earthy sadly. 'It cut her up cruel inside. She were never the same again. I'd not fancy chiny.'

'I like Indian best myself,' agreed Mrs Dollit. 'There's nothing like a good strong cup of Indian tea, is there? I expect you'd like some home-made cakes, too. I made them myself, so I know they're good.'

As neither of the scarecrows answered, Mrs Dollit smiled, nodded, and returned to the house.

'She's daft to think we're cows,' muttered Gummidge. 'Cows eats linseed cakes. I'd not demean myself.'

He jerked the fingers of one wash-leather glove among the tea-things until they rattled.

'What's them?' he asked.

'Cups and saucers and plates,' Robin told him. 'You put the tea in the cups and you put the cups on the saucers. The cakes go on the plates.'

'Things as isn't daft – things like pigs and ducks – drinks sensible out o' troughs and ponds. They washes in what they drinks, and they drinks in what they washes in. Stands to reason.'

Earthy spoke thoughtfully. 'I don't know as I could abide to drink like a duck, Worzel. Very undignified eatin' and drinkin' upside-down must be. If you're used to swallerin' down, you'd need a lot o' comfortin' arterwards if you started swallerin' up, same as ducks does. I've allus thought as ducks' stummicks did ought to be above their heads for comfort, though it wouldn't look smart.'

She broke off suddenly, and pointed with a red gloved finger. 'Oh, Worzel, love! Did ever you see such a poor bird?'

Somehow, the parrot had managed to open the door of its cage. Now it was sidling over the grass towards the tea-table. Every now and then it paused, raised a spread-about grey claw, and scratched its head.

'It's the parrot,' said Robin.

'There's no such bird!' argued Gummidge. 'Stands to reason there's not!'

The parrot came nearer, blinked a grey eye at the scare-crow, and screeched 'Pretty Polly!'

'I'll not be shouted names at by no bird that's not a bird! I'll scare it!'

Worzel Gummidge raised a broomstick arm, set the sleeve of Captain Conway's raincoat flapping, and shouted, 'Shoo!'

'It isn't calling you names, it's saying its own,' explained Robin as the raincoat's cuff sent a teacup spinning to the grass.

'Pretty Polly!' said the parrot.

'You said its name were PARROT.'

'Yes, but all parrots are called POLLY.'

Earthy interrupted. 'Did ever you see a poor bird in such need o' comfortin'? Look at its poor grey feet and its grey hooked beak and its poor red tail!'

'Pretty Polly!' repeated the parrot.

'Oh, Worzel, love, to think the poor thing thinks it's pretty!'

Earthy's voice was warm with pity – 'To think it might 'a' been hatched out real pretty like a chick bird. What's its mother thinkin' not to be comfortin' it?'

'I expect its mother's in Africa,' said Robin.

'The very idea! Fancy flyin' off to foreign parts and leavin' this poor thing to get along with strangers!'

'Cuckoos does!' argued Gummidge.

'That shows what foreign travel does to birds' hearts. Cuckoos is eddicate to know as other silly lovin' birds'll sit on its eggs for it – that's what eddication does. A silly lovin' bird like a hen'll go on sittin' and hopin' on addled eggs.'

'It looks like this bird come out o' addled eggs – lots o' differ ones,' said Gummidge.

'Pretty Polly!' yelled the parrot defiantly, and it half stalked, half sidled under the tea-table, where it stayed happily for a time, tweaking the fringe of the tartan rug.

This was just as well because Mrs Dollit came out of the house again. She was carrying a tray which held a teapot and a plate of iced cakes. Worzel Gummidge glared at them suspiciously, but Earthy looked proud and pleased.

Perhaps Mrs Dollit might have asked for payment but just then a strange man came into the garden, and she bustled towards him.

The man was wearing a tightly-fitting rather shiny dark blue suit. He had a red face and a red tie. His shoes were very well polished, and he took off his cap when Mrs Dollit spoke to him.

Robin could not hear what was said, but presently Mrs Dollit went back into the house and the man strolled over to a tea-table near to Saucy Nancy. This was rather a nuisance because Robin had hoped to have more conversation with the figurehead.

Earthy was stroking a pink iced cake with the forefinger of one of her woollen gloves. Gummidge was lowering his mouth towards the teapot's hot spout.

'I'd better pour out for you,' said Robin hastily.

'Thankee, my dear.' Earthy smiled politely as the boy slopped tea and milk into the cups, and spooned in as much sugar as he would have liked himself.

But how were the scarecrows to drink? Robin was quite sure they would not be able to grip cup-handles. They might be able to manage lemonade straws, but lemonade was not sold at *The Treasure Ship*.

Two words came into his mind – *bottle-straws*. Worzel Gummidge was wearing his boots, though these were hidden by the rug. Robin dived under the table to the annoyance of the parrot, who hurried away. He tweaked twice, and then stood up – a bottle-straw in each hand.

The straws were bent, battered and slightly muddy, but he knew that the scarecrows were not particularly fussy.

Worzel Gummidge was sniffing at the steamy tea.

'It smells worse nor the rick in Farmer Braithewaite's yard arter rain,' he grumbled.

Earthy had made a sort of porridge of tea and iced cake in her cup, and was stirring it with a glove-finger.

Robin dumped a straw into each cup.

'Now, SUCK!' he said.

Earthy did her obedient best. She blew downwards till the 'porridge' bubbled. There was a slushy gurgling sound from her husband's cup, and then a silence. Robin's own experience told him that the straw had bent badly in the middle. He had done his best but what should he do next?

From across the garden the voice of the stranger hailed him heartily –

'Hi! Boy! Come here!'

# 9 The Sea-Faring Man

The man was sitting under one of the big orange umbrellas, but Robin decided that he did not look used to umbrellas. His face was weatherbeaten and his eyes were very blue. He had a way of screwing them up as though he were trying to see far, far into the distance.

''Morning, boy,' he said. 'My name's Perkins.'

'Good morning. Mine's Robin Elliot.'

'I thought I heard a parrot talking early this forenoon.'

'There!' Robin admired the man's quick speech, and tried to imitate it. 'There!'

He pointed to the parrot which was slowly making its way across the grass, and stopping every now and then to scratch its head or to peck contemptuously at the gnomes' feet.

'Pretty Polly!' squawked the bird.

'It wasn't talking like that early in the forenoon,' said Mr Perkins. 'I stepped into the garden to listen.'

By now, the parrot had reached the edge of Saucy Nancy's fishing-net skirt. It gripped one of the lower meshes, then up it went, claw over claw, until it reached the figure-head's shoulder.

'If that doesn't beat the band!'

Mr Perkins spoke in a loud carrying voice. The parrot blinked at him, and sidled a little way along Nancy's out-stretched arm. Then moving its claws up and down in time to the tune, it sang hoarsely:

'Oh, do you know the Sampan man, the Sampan man,
    the Sampan man?

Oh, do you know the Sampan man who lives in Wei-
    Hei Harbour?'

Mr Perkins slapped his thick leg, and roared with
laughter.

'If that bird doesn't know the China Station, I'm a
lascar! That's a fine figurehead, too. She's seen some days!
I'll be bound she's seen some days!'

There was a chink of crockery, a rattle of teaspoons, and
Mrs Dollit put a tray on the table. The scent of steaming
coffee, hot milk and freshly iced cakes mingled with the
drift of very old fishing-net.

Mr Perkins pulled a handful of silver from his pocket,
and flung it down on a plate. (So, thought Robin, might a
pirate have spilled pieces of eight all over a blood-soaked
deck. He was liking Mr Perkins more and more.)

'How much?'

'The cakes are fourpence each,' replied Mrs Dollit, 'and
the coffee is two shillings. I expect you'd like to pay after.'

'I'll take the lot. Daresay the nipper can help me out – I
never knew a lad that couldn't. Six cakes at fourpence
each – that's two bob, and two bob for the coffee.' Mr
Perkins picked up two half-crowns, and handed them to
Mrs Dollit. 'And a bob for the washer-upper. That's a fine
figurehead you've got there. Any chance she's for sale?'

Mrs Dollit said she was sorry, and she *looked* sorry, too.
She explained that the figurehead had been a present to
her daughter, who liked to use it as a garden ornament.

'Pity!' said Mr Perkins. 'What a come-down! I reckon
the parrot's not for sale?'

Sadly, Mrs Dollit agreed that it was not.

'And that's a pity, too!' she added. 'I've never known
such an insulting bird. The disgusting things it says are

enough to put squeamish visitors off their food. I'll ask my daughter, though.'

'Tell her I can pay for my fancies.'

When Mrs Dollit had gone away, Mr Perkins spoke briefly to Robin. 'Tuck in!' he said.

The rude remarks of the parrot had no power to put the boy off his food. He ate the icing from some of the buns *first* and saved the smooth sweet tops of others to be kept for a treat at the end.

Mr Perkins only spoke once.

'Don't like sweet-stuff,' he said, and continued to stir and sip his coffee while he gazed at Saucy Nancy, and listened to her conversation with the parrot. Only Robin knew that it *was* a conversation: his companion thought he was listening to a one-bird recitation. Certainly the parrot was improving.

'Blister my barnacles! Souse me in bilge-water!' it screeched.

'Weevil-faced limpet!' roared Saucy Nancy. 'Scupper scavenger with a leech that flaps like mother's washing-day! Sea-horse with prawn-whiskers! Cargo of sago! You've shipped enough bilge to sink a porpoise.'

'Show your sea-legs, washerwoman! Show a leg! Show a leg! Show a leg!' jeered the parrot. 'Chew your fish-tail, you scum of an inshore mermaid!'

'Go and chew seaweed in Davy Jones's locker!' bellowed Saucy Nancy.

Mr Perkins finished his coffee, and wiped his mouth with the back of his hand in a way forbidden to Robin.

'Got to have that bird!' he said. 'Been a sea-going man. Always had a parrot. Think you can get round the old lady?'

For a moment Robin thought he was talking about Saucy Nancy. She, he knew, would take a great deal of 'getting round'. Then he remembered Mrs Dollit, who did not like the parrot. His feelings were mixed and his loyalties muddled. Saucy Nancy needed the parrot, and so did Mr Perkins.

Luckily his mouth was so full that he couldn't answer.

'That's right!' said Mr Perkins, 'think before you speak.'

Indoors, Miss Dollit was having an argument with her mother, who had told her about the offer for Saucy Nancy and the parrot. It was true that more money was needed to provide *The Treasure Ship* with more treasures, but she could not make up her mind to part with it, and she was quite sure that she would never sell the figurehead.

From the window she could see Saucy Nancy. The sunlight shone on the dew-spangled shawl. The painted hair was black and gleaming as a raven's wing. The arm (bare now, for the parrot had decided to visit the Gummidges' tea-table) showed a lovely curving.

'Look, Mother,' said Miss Dollit, 'that figurehead is magnificent!'

But Mrs Dollit was not looking at the figurehead, but gazing in horror at the further tea-table. There, strolling between over-turned cups, and pecking contemptuously at cakes, was the parrot. The tea-pot lay on the grass beside a broken plate, and the scarecrows were sitting very still.

As a matter of fact, Worzel Gummidge was responsible for the damage, and the parrot had only just clambered, by way of Earthy Mangold's lap, on to the table, but how was Mrs Dollit to know this. She saw the confusion, and supposed that the new visitors were offended. She was quite right about *that* because Gummidge, annoyed by the taste of tea, had fallen into one of his deadliest sulks, and Earthy, disappointed because he would not speak, was doing her best to imitate him.

Mrs Dollit snatched up a duster, and hurried out into the garden.

The parrot looked at her, scratched its head as though in puzzlement, make a noise like a hiccough, clawed a cup over, and left the table by the way it had come.

'I do apologize!' Mrs Dollit spoke to Earthy, but the little scarecrow did not reply: she was shocked that the parrot should have been treated so unkindly.

'I can't apologize enough,' said Mrs Dollit, turning to Worzel Gummidge, but he was in a dead sulk which was to last for the whole of that day.

Poor Mrs Dollit could think of nothing else to say, so she picked up the tea-pot and walked sadly back to the house. She met her daughter, who had been watching from the window, coming out of it.

'Did you see what happened?' gasped Mrs Dollit. 'I apologized to the visitors, but they didn't say a word – not one single word. They'll never come again, and they'll tell everyone.'

'Oh, no they won't, Mother, dear. They *can't* tell anyone!'

'Can't they!' said Mrs Dollit. 'I know what they'll say!'

Mr Perkins, followed by Robin, strolled up to the mother and daughter, and spoke at exactly the right moment.

'About that parrot? How'd it be if I took it on approval?'

His hand went to his pocket and pulled out two pretty-looking five-pound notes.

'Can't expect you to trust me. Stranger to you. I've a caravan on the new site.'

'Well —' said Miss Dollit, glancing at the notes, and looking away, 'I don't think —'

The parrot was tweaking the tip of one of the gnome's red plaster shoes. It tweaked again, and the tip broke off in its beak.

'Well, yes,' sighed Miss Dollit.

So it was arranged. Ten minutes later, after a great deal of rufflement and squawking and pecking, the parrot was swinging in its cage and the cage was swinging from Mr Perkins's big broad hand as he walked out of the garden.

Mrs Dollit went back into the house, so did Miss Dollit

after she had tidied up the scarecrows' tea-table, shaken the crumbs from Earthy Mangold's cardigan, and pulled a long bent straw from between Worzel Gummidge's turnipy lips. The straw puzzled her.

Robin went back to the sundial, and sat cross-legged beside it, waiting for Saucy Nancy to speak first.

When she did speak it was in a sad gruff voice.

'I was getting used to that bird!'

Robin guessed that she meant she had been getting fond of it. So he had spoken of his first knife – the one with the cork-screw, and of a London sparrow that he had rescued (just too late) from a cat.

He looked up shyly, and rather expected to see a crusty tear shining dryly under the figurehead's left eye, but what he *did* see startled him.

The whole of her face glistened, the outstretched arm shone with moisture, and as he watched something like a dew-drop fell from the pointing finger.

*She looks like Mary Lou's doll did the night she'd been left out in the garden and it started to freeze,* thought Robin, *but there hasn't been a frost. There was dew on her nets before – it can't be that, and she can't be crying all over!*

As though he had spoken his thoughts aloud, Saucy Nancy answered, but still in the same choked voice.

'It's the salt water working out of my system – that's all it is, young shaver. Fair pickled in brine I am. Whenever I see a sea-faring man, the salt works out of my system. I was getting used to that parrot!'

*I know what she means all right,* thought Robin, *I know what she means. If she was Mary Lou I could pick her up and laugh her out of it. But Saucy Nancy's up already. I don't know what to say.*

'Sea-faring man, he was,' repeated Saucy Nancy. 'The reek of his baccy put me in mind of home.'

'Do you mean the sea?' asked Robin.

'O' course I mean the sea. Sea's home to sea-farers.'

'Sorry about the parrot!' muttered Robin.

'There's other birds than parrots. Never mind parrots!'

A blackbird perched on Nancy's finger but only for a moment because she jerked it off.

'Get away, worm-eater, I've known better birds than you, I have! I've had swallows perched all over me when they was resting on the flight to Afriky. AND I've seen the Albatross! Get away!'

Then in a voice that reminded Robin of a gentle wind stirring among the new leaves of trees, the figurehead sang –

> 'Oh! little folk who live on land
> And count your gain – I count your loss,
> A loss you cannot understand
> Who have not seen the Albatross
> Skimming the air on stately wing,
> While on the sea the ripples fling
> Into a silver blossoming –
> A flowering of sudden Spring.

> 'The Albatross has wings as pale
> As summer clouds in azure sky,
> It sets each wing to make a sail
> And, as the sea-miles scurry by –
> Some seven hundred in a day
> (Or so believing sailors say) –
> It floats in its unhurried way
> From spar to stay
> And far away.'

The tune died away, and Nancy spoke. 'She's got a lot wrong o' course. She didn't know a spar from a stay.'

'Who didn't?' asked Robin.

'The skipper's missus – the one that put the words together. She was allus hanging over the side looking for mermaids, but she *liked* the albatross.'

Saucy Nancy raised her voice again –

> 'My thoughts have flown so high and far
> (So far away, so long ago)
> Beyond the dim horizon's bar
> Where Southern winds and waters flow.
> They do not gather lubber's moss
> Or ever reckon gain or loss
> Who've sailed beneath the Southern Cross
> Where high winds toss
> The Albatross.'

The singing ended. Nancy jerked a drop of brine from her finger-tip, and said, 'Aye! There's better birds nor parrots, but parrots *is* sea-faring in a way.'

The words decided Robin. He would go to the caravan site, find Mr Perkins and beg him *not* to like the parrot, but he would not tell Nancy about his plan just in case it failed.

'Aye!' repeated Nancy, 'I've seen worse nor parrots come out o' ditty-bags.'

'What's a ditty-bag?' asked Robin.

'It's what seamen stow their gear in, landlubber. I could tell you a yarn about that.'

Robin settled himself to listen.

'We were in harbour at the time, and my old skipper – the one with the wooden leg – saw a new cabin boy coming aboard with his ditty-bag. He was off another ship, and he'd a bundle, tied up in a red knotted handkercher, in his other hand. "What's that you're carrying?" asked the skipper. The boy put the handkercher behind his back. Then he answered, all pert and holystoned – "Ditty-bag. Ain't yer seen one o' them before?" The skipper spoke gentle as a winkle, "Ho! Ditty-bags hold ditties, and ditties is nursery rhymes. Them that carries ditty-bags has to answer in rhyme – that's the rule in this ship. If you don't answer in rhyme you'll be touched up with a rope's-end till you do!" The cabin boy smirked and stood ready. "Now then," says the skipper, "if I ask you – *What's eight bells mean*? How'd you answer me in rhyme?" The boy scratched his head a bit. Then he piped up:

> "Ding-dong bell,
> Pussy's in the well."

'At that the skipper was so tummy-come-flustered (and I won't say he hadn't tom-cat whiskers) he tipped backwards into the drink. The cabin boy leaned over the rails, all gentle and innocent-like, and he piped up:

> "Who pulled him out?
> Little Tommy Trout."

'The skipper's sea-boots were filling with water, and his whiskers were awash. The cabin boy scratched his head some more. Then he bawled:

> "My name's Willy Penny,
> And I'm not saving ANY!"

'So the skipper was drownded and I near bust my seams laughing when he spun me the yarn in the dog-watch. "That boy'll be skipper yet!" he shouted. Then he forgot his wooden leg, and stamped with that hard as with tother!'

Saucy Nancy laughed hoarsely.

'But,' said Robin doubtfully, 'if the skipper was drowned, how could he tell you? Oh! —'

'You got to learn to sort the spindrift from the yarn!' cackled Saucy Nancy.

Robin thought of asking what spindrift *was*, but he didn't like being laughed at. He could find out from Mr Perkins.

'Got to go home to dinner,' he said, and strolled away.

As he was passing the scarecrow's tea-table, Earthy Mangold stretched out her red glove, and patted him.

'I've been tryin' to talk tea-table talk to Mr Gummidge,'

she said. 'Upsidaisy told me folks as sits at tea-tables did ought to talk tea-table talk, but I casn't get him interested.'

Worzel Gummidge looked very sulky indeed. He was staring down at his wash-leather gloves. A spider was spinning a web between a finger and thumb.

'I was tellin' him about a friend o' mine as happened to be stuffed with pilly feathers.'

'Why?' asked Robin.

'Well you've got to be stuffed with sommat else you sags. As I was sayin' I wanted some feather trimmin' for me new hat. It were made out o' an old saucepan. Ever so smart it were the way the handle stuck out one side.'

Robin fidgeted because he so hated talk about fashions, but he didn't like to shake Earthy's hand from his sleeve.

'I happened to have dipped that hat in tar they was mendin' the roads with, and I went up to my friend – her name was Tilly Tinfoot acos she happened to have bully-beef-tin ankle socks – and I asked for a lend o' some o' her feathers. She turned all mean, and told me to look in a hen-yard when hens was moultin'. Then I noticed the weakness o' her stummick where they'd patched it with curtain net so the feathers was stickin' out, and then —'

Earthy stopped, and Robin noticed that her potato-ish cheeks had turned green. The little scarecrow was blushing.

'I didn't mean no harm,' she continued. 'The feathers'd have blowed away anyway, but I laid my hat agin the weakness o' her stummick, and lots o' the feathers stuck to the tar, so I got me trimmin', but some o' the tar from my hat gave her a black stummick. I'll never forgive mesel' not but what Upsidaisy says black stummicks is fashionable in foreign parts. She's seen picters o' black stummicks in school books – lots o' black stummicks and the folks as has 'em. She says they looks ever so happy.'

The woollen gloved hand quivered pathetically on Robin's sleeve.

'It wouldn't 'a' mattered so much about Tilly Tinfoot's stummick bein' black if all them white butterflies hadn't stuck to it. Tilly happened to be courtin' at the time – courtin' a very smart scarecrow with marble eyes. They got on beautiful lovin' till the butterflies come but HE said he didn't fancy the idea of a wife that had a black stummick trimmed with butterflies. He said folks might think she weren't partickler.'

Green tears rolled down Earthy's greenly blushing cheeks.

'So Tilly Tinfoot's still spinstering. So smart she used to be, too, with her tin ankle socks, and door-mat cloak, and hair made out o' coconut mattin', and one red cheek where she'd lain against a paint-pot. When I thinks o' her still spinsterin' and all my fault, I wonders if I ought to let her marry Mr Gummidge and me go back to spinsterin'?'

As though he were answering in his sulk, Worzel Gummidge shook his head slowly but very firmly.

Earthy smiled, and the smile sent the tears hurrying from her cheeks. The lamb, doing for once the right thing at the right time, came bleating out of the orchard. It skipped up to Earthy.

'Ma-aa! Ma-aa! Ma-maa!' it bleated.

'You'd best leave us be, love,' said Earthy. 'Me and Lamb-love and Worzel's got to get on with the tea-table talk.'

As Robin left the garden, he heard the voice of Saucy Nancy raised in song –

> 'When wind says *Yes* and tide says *Yes*
> I glide to port like a fair princess.
> When wind says *Yes* and the tide says *No*,
> I beat to harbour – even so.
> When wind says *No* and tide says *Yes*,
> I make the harbour none the less.
> When wind says *No* and tide says *No*,
> I fight to port like Billy-oh!'

That settled it, he would find Mr Perkins now. Dinner could wait. He was full of cakes on the top of apple pasty. His mother would understand: she was an understanding mother.

The caravan site was a waste piece of ground belonging to Farmer Braithewaite. The caravans stood in rows, and each had its own small patch of garden. Some were tidy and some were rather untidy.

It was quite easy to find the one that belonged to Mr Perkins because it was painted grey instead of green or cream, and because there was a flagpole in the garden.

Inside all was, as Mr Perkins would have said, 'all ship-shape and Bristol fashion.'

The saucepans gleamed, the floor shone, and the bunk at the far end was so tidy that the bedclothes might have been ironed on to it.

The parrot's cage hung from a hook on the ceiling, but the parrot had settled itself into a grey huff. Every now and then it plucked out a feather, gripped it in a claw, and nibbled the quill end.

A rich smell of stew and herbs rose from a pot on the oil stove, and made Robin forget that he was not hungry.

'Never liked eating alone,' said Mr Perkins as he spooned stew on to two plates. 'Set-to, shaver!'

He put the plates on to the table, and handed Robin a spoon and a hunk of bread.

'Don't believe in wasting good gravy,' he said.

'Pretty Polly!' remarked the parrot, pulling out another feather and throwing away the chewed one.

Robin, as he wolfed the stew, wondered how he could explain about Saucy Nancy's misery. Mr Perkins had paid for the parrot, and Miss Dollit had the money. He need not have troubled because as the bird repeated 'Pretty Polly!' Mr Perkins pushed aside his own plate, plumped both his elbows on to the table, and said –

'About that bird, see – it's moping. Watch it.'

The parrot jerked out another feather, nibbled it, let it fall, and settled into a grey huff again. It looked the very picture of 'mope'.

'Bored – that's what it is – bored with me.'

Robin thought it strange that anything should be bored by Mr Perkins and his lovely caravan, but he did not say so.

'That's why it's pulling out its feathers – to give itself something to do. Bird could pluck itself clean as a bosun's whistle in a coupla days.

'Bored parrots pluck themselves . . . That bird's no use to me nor I to it . . . Bored and sentimental . . . Been on at me to kiss it . . . Been Pretty-Pollying ever since I brought it back.'

'Pretty Polly! Kiss poor Polly!' said the parrot, and pulled out another feather.

'Pretty Polly!' Mr Perkins blew out a great puff of smoke from his pipe, 'It didn't keep on Pretty-Pollying this fore-noon. Ask me, it's pining for the figurehead . . . I said I'd take it on appro: . . . Good thing I did . . . You'd best take it back before it plucks itself clean . . . Take it back, boy.'

'What about the money if Miss Dollit isn't in?' asked Robin.

Mr Perkins slapped the table so hard that the plates bounced, and the parrot, startled out of its huff, exclaimed, 'Kiss poor Polly!'

'Money! I don't want money!'

Robin was startled, too. All the people he knew wanted money, some of them very badly.

Mr Perkins puffed at his pipe again. 'I'm made of money . . . Just won twenty thousand on a football pool . . . Cool twenty thousand . . . Said I could pay for me fancies . . . I've got my eye on a little public house down Pompey way . . . Name of *The Three Feathers*.' He laughed, 'There'd be a sight more than three feathers if that parrot keeps on the

way it's doing . . . I want a bird that'll chat to the customers
the way they're used to . . . Not THAT bird . . . Sailors
don't want Pretty-Pollying. I'd be a laughing stock in my
own tap-room if that bird kept shouting me to kiss it . . .
Wouldn't I?'

Robin nodded, not because his mouth was too full for
speech, but because he was disappointed that Mr Perkins
was not going to stay in Scatterbrook.

'Not going yet . . . You can look me up when next you
come to Pompey . . . Pompey's short for Portsmouth . . .
I've a mind to buy a racing dinghy when I get down there
. . . You might like to come for a sail next time you come
to Pompey.'

*Next time I come to Pompey!* thought Robin. *He talks as
though I was a man. I will come to Pompey, I will.*

'Thanks,' he said.

'Pleasure!' said Mr Perkins, taking down the cage. 'And
now, skedaddle before that bird finishes its strip-tease act.'

'Kiss poor Polly,' murmured the parrot.

Mr Perkins took four (yes FOUR) half-crowns from a
shelf, and pushed them into the pocket of Robin's shorts.

'Always tip the porter!' he said. 'Bird'll be all right now
. . . Wish I could've bought that figurehead . . . Off you
go! . . . Skedaddle! . . . See you in Pompey next time
you're there . . . So long!'

Miss Dollit was *in* when Robin reached *The Treasure Ship*
but she was just going out. As well as he could, Robin explained what had happened. As well as *she* could, because
she was excited about a new plan, Miss Dollit listened.

'Are you quite sure that Mr Perkins doesn't want his
money back?' she asked.

'No, he said he was made of money,' Robin told her.

'Then put the parrot into the garden, but don't let it
out of its cage just yet. Be as quiet as you can because my
mother is resting upstairs. Now I must fly!'

Worzel Gummidge and Earthy were sitting at their tea-table. The lamb seemed to have taken a dislike to one of the gnomes, and was doing its best to push it over. Saucy Nancy pointed from her sundial. Nothing had changed except that the sun was much higher in the sky.

'Here's the parrot,' said Robin, as he hung the cage in the apple-tree.

'Dip your finger in bilge-water and write home to mother!' exclaimed Saucy Nancy. 'I'd got used to that bird, young shaver!'

Robin was quite obedient. He did NOT open the cage-door: the parrot showed off the trick it had learned in the morning. In no time at all, or in no more time than it might have taken a thrush to fly backwards across the garden, Nancy's bird was perched on Nancy's arm.

'Well, weevil face!' she said lovingly.

'Pickled pilchard!' screamed the parrot, and sidled along the figurehead's forearm till it reached the finger. Then it raised a grey claw as though in salute, and winked at Robin.

Saucy Nancy raised her rusty voice in song –

'When first I set to sea, young nipper,
  Me eyes were brighter blue –
I sailed the Flood with a rorty skipper
  When Noah's Ark was new.
The stowaway horses started neighing,
  And Noah he said, said he,
"So long as they do what I keep saying,
  They'll sail along o' we!"
    But they wouldn't go WHOA!
    For Father Noah;
    They wouldn't go GEE!
    For me –
So we tipped 'em over
Where there weren't no clover
    In the big blue fields of sea.'

*I wonder*, thought Robin, *I wonder if she's singing to me? I'm the only nipper here. Mr Perkins called me a nipper.*

He had forgotten the parrot. The bird was numbling Nancy's finger, nipping it in the most loving way. The figurehead continued her song –

'When next you watch the sea, young nipper,
     Remember Saucy Nan,
The stowaway nags and the rorty skipper,
     And catch as-catch-you can
Those runaway nags with white manes streaming,
     And tails that lash the spray;
But never you think you've caught me dreaming
     When the pounding hoof-beats say –
          Our sires said WHOA!
     To Father Noah,
          And our dams said GEE!
          To he –
          And we won't climb over
          The cliffs of Dover
     Because we belong to sea.'

*So'll I belong to the sea*, thought Robin, *AND I'll go to sea and have my own parrot.*

The four half-crowns felt warm and heavy in his pocket. He chinked them together as he walked home.

## 10 The Badger-Badgerer

It was a damp drizzling morning. If it had not been for the change in the weather, Worzel Gummidge and Earthy Mangold might still have been sitting under the orange umbrella, and 'enjoying' a tea-party. But Miss Dollit had promised to take care of the clothes she had borrowed from Captain Conway.

So now, Worzel Gummidge, gloveless, scarfless, and wearing his own old hat, stood in the painted drain-pipe outside the summer-house. Inside it, Earthy Mangold was 'drying off'. The lamb was with her, and the parrot's cage hung from the rustic woodwork.

Rain had made the garden very peaceful.

Inside *The Treasure Ship*, Marlene was being busy and important. She had had a glorious round of the Scatterbrook dustbins, and retrieved a tin nearly full of gold paint (thrown away by Mrs Bloomsbury-Barton) and nine scallop shells (remnants of a dinner-party given by Mrs Conway). Now the shells had been gilded, and were to be sold as ashtrays. Marlene was arranging them on a little table, while Mrs Dollit tidied the antique shop.

Robin was there, too, because he had crept into the garden to visit Saucy Nancy, had been seen by sensible Mrs Dollit, and called in out of the rain.

Now he stood, hands in his pockets, and wondered what to do. One of his pockets felt rich because of the four half-crowns. The other one bulged heavily because it was full of smooth oval stones that had been turned up by the plough. His father was making a cobblestone path between the gate and front door of Finch Cottage, and had asked Robin to collect stones of the right shape and size.

'This shell needs another dab of paint,' said Marlene, whisking the lid off the paint-tin and then licking the brush.

'Next time I find some shells I'm going to make little velvet pincushions to stick between them – oyster-coloured velvet so they'll look like fish.'

'What a good idea!' exclaimed Miss Dollit, and her mother remarked that though she had heard of people eating winkles with a pin, she could see no reason why anyone should mistake scallops for oysters or use either as pincushions.

Miss Dollit sighed, and so did Robin – not because he minded what Marlene did, but because he felt out of things. *The Treasure Ship* wasn't a ship – there was no real treasure – only pencils with hats, and horse-brasses (*Who, but a horse, would want a horse-brass, and horses don't go shopping*) and all the silly things that had been painted or shaped to look like other silly things.

The *sight* of the gold paint and the *feeling* of the stones in his pocket gave him an idea.

*Nuggets*, he thought, *gold nuggets and buried treasure. We could paint the stones and bury them and watch people digging them up. Pity the first of April's over.*

He whispered to Marlene, and in another few minutes he and she were squatting by the big fireplace. The stones were spread out on a newspaper, and they were taking it in turns to use the brush.

Mrs Dollit continued to dust and to mutter until the front door opened, and a thin rather anxious-looking man came into the shop. His neck was long and scraggy, and he wore dark glasses, and was dressed very tidily.

'Forgive me for asking,' he said. 'This doesn't *look*

that kind of shop but I wonder if you happen to sell clothes.'

'Not ordinary clothes, I'm afraid,' replied Miss Dollit. 'I have a few period costumes, and there's a very jolly Roumanian peasant's outfit. Where is it, Mother?'

Mrs Dollit waved her feather duster.

'Over there, isn't it, covering that case of stuffed birds?'

Miss Dollit darted across the shop. 'Yes, here it is!'

She shook out an embroidered tunic, and a pair of baggy white trousers. 'The colours of the embroidery are exciting, aren't they?'

The man shook his scrawny neck, and answered sadly, 'Yes, but I'm afraid they would be too exciting for badgers. The fact is I am looking for *old* clothes.'

Robin glanced up from his painting. Perhaps this unlikely looking visitor would turn out to be another man after his own heart.

Miss Dollit looked offended. 'We sell antiques,' she said, 'not ordinary old clothes.'

'Quite! Quite!' the man spoke quickly. 'I should have explained myself better. I am lecturing tomorrow to a Field Club. They call themselves the Friends of Fur, Fin and Feather.'

Mrs Dollit snorted.

'Tonight I am to go badger-watching in the woods –' (COO, thought Robin). 'Unfortunately I left my bag in the train – the bag containing my Field Club clothes – a very ragged old suit in which it would be impossible to travel. Field Club work is ruination to clothes' – (he looked down at his own neatly-pressed trousers) – 'because of the brambles and the damp. I have taken a room at *The Red Lion* in case the weather should be too impossible. I only wondered – it was just an idea –'

The newly-installed telephone rang, and Miss Dollit

leaped to answer it –

'Scatterbrook 209!' she said. 'Yes, we have a tea-garden
... Tomorrow? Yes, we shall be delighted ... No, not
farmhouse teas, dainty teas ... Yes, DAINTY teas ...
For twelve ... Yes, I'll repeat it – THE FUR, FIN and
FEATHER FRIENDS ... Punctually at four o'clock?
... Yes, thank you very much. Good-bye ... Oh, thirteen
altogether.'

She hung up the receiver.

'I fancy that must have been the Secretary of the Fur, Fin
and Feather Society,' said the stranger. 'I am supposed to
join them, and give them the result of my wild life night
watching. I can't imagine what this suit will look like by
tomorrow.'

'There's an old clothes shop in Dimden,' put in Mrs
Dollit, but her daughter, delighted by the thought of such
a large tea-party, had another idea.

'Old Man Scarecrow!' she cried, and because her visitor
looked startled, she explained, 'I didn't mean you, Mr –
Mr —?'

'Wood is the name,' he answered. 'Really, it is rather
suitable, as I spend so much of my time in wet woods.'

Miss Dollit laughed delightedly.

'I can let you have some scarecrow clothes, Mr Wood.
I've a splendid Old Man Scarecrow in the summer-house.
I'll show you, and you can change there.'

'Shall I help?' asked Robin, thinking that he might have
a chance of begging to go on the badger-watching expedi-
tion.

'No! No, I must explain to Mr Wood.'

Miss Dollit and her visitor bustled out into the rain, and
the children were left to finish their painting.

The nuggets looked glorious to Robin, but Marlene began
to complain as the paint in the tin sank lower and lower
and the newspaper became splattered with golden blobs.

'Don't put it on so thick,' she said. 'I'll need most of the rest of the paint.'

'Whaffor?' asked Robin.

'I've a black satin cushion cover at home. It's got rubbed through, and it's got tinsel bands and tassels. I want to make them gold again.'

*Tinsel bands and cushions!* In his mind, Robin had been exploring an island inhabited only by himself and Saucy Nancy and the parrot and Mr Perkins. The nuggets had become real to him. They were buried with a hoard of pieces of eight and uncut rubies beside the bones of a pirate. Marlene's words brought him whizzing home.

'Cushions are silly!' he said.

Marlene didn't answer for a time. She was rubbing the backs of her nails on to the blobs of paint. Now she licked round the edges, and spread her fingers out to dry. She had read in a magazine that 'smart' people sometimes used gold and silver lacquer on their nails instead of ordinary red stuff.

'It's silly to waste paint on silly old stones,' she said, and, still keeping her fingers apart, she dropped the lid on to the tin, and pressed it down with her elbow.

'You'd better wash your hands *well* before you eat anything,' remarked Mrs Dollit.

Marlene, with the tin tucked under her arm and the paint-brush in her mouth, whisked out of the front door just as Miss Dollit returned from the garden.

'I've left Mr Wood to change,' she said. 'Old Man Scarecrow's clothes ought to fit him beautifully. He *is* such an interesting man. He's going up to the woods now to find a good hiding-place.'

'Then he must be out of his mind!' Mrs Dollit spoke severely. 'The idea of a man of his age playing hide-and-seek in damp woods.'

'Oh, Mother, dear, you don't understand. Mr Wood must hide himself from the badgers and other creatures so that *he* can watch them without *them* seeing him. He's going up to the woods again at seven o'clock this evening, and he'll stay there all night. Then he'll have a long sleep, and be ready to talk to the Fur, Fin and Feather Society at four o'clock tomorrow afternoon. I'm so glad, for his sake, that it has stopped raining.'

Mrs Dollit, murmuring that she must see if there was enough lard for cake-making, bustled into the kitchen, and Robin tried to cover the nuggets with a spare sheet of newspaper. He was too late: Miss Dollit had seen them.

'What a lovely idea!' she cried. 'A surprise for me, are they?'

Robin did not answer because it would have been difficult to say that the nuggets were not for Miss Dollit.

He looked on while she arranged the gilded stones in a glass bowl, put it in the window, and sprinkled some imitation pearls from a broken necklace on the ledge beside it.

'There!' she said. 'Treasure for *The Treasure Ship*! Thank you, Robin. Now shall we tidy up these newspapers?'

*Treasure should be hidden,* thought Robin, *or treasure should be buried on an island by a pirate's bones.*

Sunlight streamed suddenly through the window, the nuggets shone like real gold and the mock pearls gleamed.

Suddenly nothing mattered, except that the rain had stopped. He could visit Saucy Nancy and the Scarecrows, and he could work out his new plan.

Mr Wood had not troubled to return Worzel Gummidge to his drain-pipe. The scarecrow stood propped against the summer-house window, and looking very odd indeed. He was bare-headed except for his sprouting turnip-top hair, and he looked much thinner than usual. This was because Mr Wood had bundled him into Captain Conway's raincoat which had been hung up to dry – the cap, gloves and scarf had been taken indoors by Miss Dollit.

Except for the coat, and this had not been buttoned, Gummidge wore nothing but his bottle-straw boots, faded shirt and tarred string-braces. Mr Wood's dark blue suit was folded neatly, and shared a deck chair with his bowler hat.

'Pretty Polly!' said the parrot admiringly.

Earthy was trying to comfort her husband.

'They do say exchange is no robbery,' she said. 'Arter all, Worzel, the genelman's left his clothes for you. Beggin' his pardon, and if it's all the same to him, it would 'a' been perliter to have put 'em on you, and not left you standin' in your sticks.'

'I'd not demean mesel' to wear his clothes – not till I've give 'em a good rollin' and rakin',' grunted Gummidge. 'Ooh aye, a good rakin' through a barb fence or a good roll with a harrow'd make all the differ. Very iggerant about clothes humans is.'

'I'd never 'a' thought as though the genelman's clothes'd take off, seein' his face put me in mind o' a genelman scarecrow as chanced to be a friend o' mine,' said Earthy. 'A very sad case his was – a very sad case indeed. He looked so smart in his sacking suit afore it happened.'

'What happened?' asked Robin rathèr quickly, because he was afraid that Earthy might burst into tears.

'He happened to come on an old suit laying in the hedge, but it were too small for him, so he thought, maybe, he'd take his own suit off of him afore he put tother on.'

'That were a daft thing to do,' interrupted Gummidge.

'People *do* take off their suits before putting other suits on,' said Robin.

'Not if they're stuffed with old twitch grass they shouldn't,' explained Earthy, 'and not if the twitch grass'd sprouted in the rain, and rooted into the suit. This genelman scarecrow friend o' mine chanced to be stuffed with twitch grass. When a genelman takes his suit off and most o' the genelman comes off with the suit, he'll have a job to look the same again. We did what we could with sheep-nettin' but he

were more or less o' an invalid arter that. I'm glad Mr
Gummidge's stuffin' rustles loose and free and easy.'

As though to make sure that it did, Worzel Gummidge
shook himself. Then he remarked, 'The genelman as took
my clothes had another suit underneath.'

'Yes,' agreed Earthy eagerly. 'It were ever so interestin'
watchin'. He'd a white shirt, and another little coat without sleeves, and long white trousies.'

'Pants and a waistcoat,' murmured Robin, but Worzel
Gummidge looked at him scornfully. 'They was cricket
trousies,' he said. 'I've watched lots o' them wearin'
trousies like that on the village green.'

'He didn't take 'em off of him,' put in Earthy. 'Maybe
he'd heard the gossip about my genelman scarecrow friend.
Maybe he were stuffed with twitch grass or buttercup –
they've shocking clingy roots.'

'Anyways,' said Gummidge, 'he's daft. Nobody as wasn't
daft'd call 'emsel's Wood when they're not made o' wood
nor don't look like a wood. He's stole my clothes and he's
gone prying about in the wood, disturbin' things that wants
to go to sleep and interferin' with things that wants to
catch their dinners. I'll learn the moles to learn him a
lesson. Ooh aye! Stands to reason.'

'What sort of lesson?' asked Robin.

'A lesson as'll learn him not to go badger-badgerin' and
bird-watchin' in my trousies. Clothes is as clothes does. If
you was to dress a sheep like a hen —'

Earthy interrupted, 'Oh, Worzel, love, there'd not be
enough feathers off of one little hen to cover a great big
sheep – only in tufty patches, and if the hen were three
parts moulted, the sheep'd need a lot o' comfortin'.'

'If you was to dress a sheep like a hen, maybe it'd stop
thinkin' woolly,' argued Gummidge. 'Clothes is as clothes
does. Those that wears woolly thinks woolly. Those that
wears feathers acts flighty. Frogs dresses skiddy and they

acts skiddy. Slugs oozes slow. If you was to dress a centipede in slug-skin —'

Earthy burst into a flood of green tears, and sobbed –

'Oh, Worzel, love, I casn't abide it! To think o' a centipede in slug-skin, oozing slow and thinkin' slow, and all its legs in a skedaddle hurry. The things you think!'

'Ooh AYE! That badger-badgerer'll be thinkin' what I think, seein' he's in my trousies.'

'Nobody casn't think same as you think, Worzel, love, but if trousies makes the differ maybe you did ought to try to think the same as him – exchange bein' no robbery.'

Earthy shook off her red woollen glove. Her twiggy fingers felt warm and spring-like as they scrabbled Robin's wrist.

'Please to put Mr Gummidge into the genelman's clothes,' she begged. 'He bein' so stiff it makes it a'k'ard.'

But Worzel Gummidge, now much stiffer than before, had fallen into a sulk, and Robin, who had never found it easy to dress his little sister's dolls, guessed that the dressing of a scarecrow would be much more difficult. Besides, his inside clock told him that dinner at Finch Cottage must be very nearly ready. Besides, he had a plan in his mind. Besides – he did not want to make trouble.

'Got to go now,' he said.

But when he was half-way down the path, he looked back.

Earthy Mangold was reaching up to put Mr Wood's bowler hat on to her husband's head.

Saucy Nancy, her shawl shining and spangled by raindrops, was singing –

> 'My name is Saucy Nan – Send a gale!
> My name is Saucy Nan – Send a gale!
> My name is Saucy Nan,
> And I'll sail as best I can,
> Following the porpoise and the whale.'

Robin would have liked to chat with her but there was food to be eaten, and he must work out his plan.

During the short walk home, he though very hard indeed: *I'll need a torch for badger-watching. I can buy one at the Post Office. I'll have to use one of Mr Perkins's half-crowns. I can't ask Mum for fear she won't let me go. I'll wait till they're asleep. I can't go down the stairs because they sleep with their doors open so that they'll hear Mary Lou if she wakes. I'll have to knot my sheets together to make a rope. I'll tie it to the bed rail and slide out of the window.*

It was a bold plan, BUT —

*It's clean sheet day. Mum won't like me to make clean sheets into a rope. I'll have to get a rope somehow. There'll be a lot to do this afternoon.*

There was much more to do that afternoon than Robin expected. His mother and father were going to Dimden, and would not be back until the half-past five bus. That might have been quite useful, but Mary Lou was put into his charge.

'Play with her nicely in the garden,' said his mother. 'Don't let her out of your sight. Don't let her go near the rubbish heap or the coal house, will you?'

'I could take her out with me,' suggested Robin.

'No, dear. I think she's got a bit of a cold coming on, and I don't trust these April days. If it should begin to rain, take her indoors at once. Promise you won't go out of the garden.'

Robin sighed and promised. Then he asked, 'You'll come straight back from the bus, won't you? The Post Office shuts at six.'

'What's the Post Office got to do with anything?' asked his father.

'I want to buy something,' said Robin.

He knew that his mother meant to be very kind when she answered, 'Whatever it is, I expect we could get it better in Dimden.'

'I want to choose myself,' said Robin, anxious that no more questions should be asked.

He was grateful when his father spoke hurriedly, 'If we don't go now, we shall miss the bus to Dimden.'

Luckily Mary Lou was in one of her very best moods. She bobbed about on the grass and picked daisies, and that gave Robin a chance to explore his father's tool-shed. Yes, there was a brand new clothes-line. He took it into the garden, and began to knot it into loops that would make footholds for the midnight climb.

Mary Lou picked a lapful of buttercups, and while she played with them Robin took the rope upstairs, and hid it in the middle of his bed. The plan was going well. It became more important, every minute, that he should see a real live badger.

At exactly twenty minutes to six, Mr and Mrs Elliot opened the gate of Finch Cottage. Mary Lou, clean as when they had left her except for a grass stain on one knee and a powdering of pollen on her little pink nose, pattered down the path to meet them.

'You *have* been a good boy!' said Robin's mother, 'I can see Mary Lou hasn't been crying.'

'Present for a good boy!' said his father, pulling a torch out of his pocket. It was a lovely one – a signalling torch. 'You can make it shine red or green or white,' explained Mr Elliot. 'I bought it in the market from a cheap-jack chap.'

'It's just what I wanted – only better.' The words burst out of Robin. 'It's what I wanted from the Post Office.'

'Well, isn't that lucky!' said Mrs Elliot comfortably. 'So you needn't go to the Post Office. I had been meaning to ask you to take this box of beads to Miss Dollit. She wants to sew them on milk covers or something. I forgot to get them last week.'

'I'll take them,' said Robin eagerly. He wanted to do something to make up to his parents for not telling them about the badger-watching.

'Good boy!' said his mother approvingly, and he wished that he felt good inside.

Miss Dollit was standing at the door of *The Treasure Ship*, and she was looking very worried indeed.

'Old Man Scarecrow's gone!' she said, taking the beads, 'and Mr Wood's clothes have gone with him. Well, I don't know if they've gone with him, but they've gone. Do you know anything about it?'

Robin shook his head.

'Because if you have dressed him up in Mr Wood's clothes, and hidden him, please say so. A joke's a joke but Mr Wood didn't look as though he'd see the funny side of anything.'

'I didn't touch his clothes,' said Robin, 'but I saw them in the summer-house this morning. I'll go and look!'

'I've looked and looked!' cried poor Miss Dollit, 'but look again if you like. If only Mr Wood were a girl I could lend him some of my clothes. How can he lecture to the Fur, Feather and Fin Society dressed like a scarecrow? How can he?'

Robin didn't answer: he was on his way to the summer-house.

Earthy was alone and the deck chair was empty.

'You've never seen Mr Gummidge look so smart!' she said. 'That genelman stood up when he took his trousies off – very a'k'ard he looked. Mr Gummidge lay down – proper and dignified – to get the trousies on. We'd a bit of a struggle acos he got both *his* legs into one trousie leg. He said tother'd make a good long pocket, and he'd manage to get about in hops, but he found that a'k'ard, so we started over again. It were worth the struggle.'

'Where is he?' asked Robin.

'Not bein' with him I casn't say,' replied Earthy reasonably, 'but he happened to mention he were goin' to chat with a lot o' moles, and learn 'em to learn that genelman to stop badgerin' badgers.'

So that was that. Robin did not think he had better linger in the summer-house because Miss Dollit, still looking very distracted, was waiting on the path.

'I suppose you didn't find the clothes?' she asked, when Robin reached her.

'They aren't there,' he said.

## 11 Fur, Fin and Feather

Robin went upstairs at eight o'clock. He took off his shoes and his jacket. Then, just as he was, he slipped between the sheets. The knotted clothes-line, hard and lumpy beside him, reminded him of the adventure to come. He had brought a book upstairs with him – an exciting story about a boy who outwitted a gang of international spies. So far as he could make out the boy in the book had no sleep at all except when he was drugged by one of the spies. If a boy in a book could keep awake for nights on end, surely he (Robin) could keep his eyes open until the church clock struck twelve times.

The pages were becoming a little bleary when his father called from the garden, 'Time you put that light out, Robin, and went to sleep!'

He clicked the electric switch beside his bed. If his mother came up, she might notice that only his jacket lay on the chair. She might shut the window which he had left wide open on purpose because the window creaked, and because he must be very quiet at midnight.

Scatterbrook church clock struck nine times. Surely it had made a mistake. It MUST be ten o'clock by now.

Robin remembered the new torch, making a lump under his pillow. Of course, he could read under the bedclothes. He tried the red light first, and it made the pages of the book look as though they had been dipped in the blood of the very worst of the spies, and the words more exciting.

Then he switched to green – a much more restful colour.

He was half asleep when he was roused by going-to-bed noises from downstairs, and he switched off the torch.

His father was locking the front door. Robin recognized the familiar chunky sound of the key turning. His mother was riddling the kitchen stove. His father was closing the shutters.

Now footsteps sounded on the creaky stairs, and paused on the landing. There was a squeaking of hinges, and Robin guessed that his parents were peeping into Mary Lou's room. He snuggled more closely under the bedclothes as the church clock struck ten times. The adventure was nearer now.

*He was climbing rigging and Saucy Nancy was singing. Down below, Mr Perkins and Mr Wood were pacing the deck. A clock struck – once, twice, three times, four times – it was queer to hear the Scatterbrook clock from so far out at sea! The rigging was warm to his touch.*

Robin jerked himself out of the dream as the clock struck for the fifth time. He pushed his tousled head from between the bedclothes, and blinked at the sunlight streaming through his bedroom window.

The clock had finished striking. It was five o'clock on a lovely spring morning.

Furiously he jumped out of bed, dragged on his jacket and pushed his feet into his shoes without bothering to undo the laces.

He supposed he was too late for badger-watching, but he might not be too late to discover what Worzel Gummidge had been saying to the moles. Anyway, now that he was awake, it would be a pity to waste such a glorious morning.

He would not need either the rope or the torch now, so he pushed them into a drawer, and then tip-toed down the stairs. The front door creaked on its hinges: in another minute Robin was running down the lane.

There was a little wood on the downs near to Ten Acre Field where Worzel Gummidge spent his working days. True it was a very small wood but there were beech trees there, and a hollow where badgers were rumoured to live.

*Coo!* thought Robin, as he reached the edge of the little wood, *I've never seen so many mole-hills in all my life. I wonder if Worzel Gummidge is here?*

Mole-hills were dotted all over the springy, spongy turf. It was difficult to put a foot between them, and Robin nearly lost a shoe. Then a bramble clutched at his sleeve as though it were trying to attract attention to something. The something was Worzel Gummidge's old hat. There it was in the middle of a cluster of mole-hills that were grouped in a circle not far from the bramble bush.

At first sight the hat looked as though it were perched on air, but that was because a little fuzz of gorse hid the view. Beyond the gorse, and to left and right of it, familiar ragged coat sleeves and wrists of polished broom handle were supported by mole-hills.

*Gummidge has shrunk,* thought Robin in horror, *and he's shrinking more.*

'Worzel Gummidge!' he shouted, forgetting that he had been taught by Earthy to address her husband as MR Gummidge, 'Worzel Gummidge!'

A voice, not exactly familiar but vaguely remembered, replied –

'Help! Help!'

Robin, jumping quickly from mole-hills that gave spongily beneath his feet, rushed round to the front of the gorse bush.

Mr Wood, no taller now, it seemed, than one of Miss Dollit's gnomes, stared at him helplessly.

Robin wondered if he had fallen into a fox-hole or rabbit warren.

'I'm bogged!' gasped Mr Wood. 'I'm bogged in a hidden marsh or else the earth round here has a quick-sand quality.'

'Coo!' said Robin, and continued to stare in amazement. Mr Wood's own arms were visible from the elbows, and he was scrabbling at loose earth and primrose roots in a way that reminded the boy of a dog's swimming action.

'Shall I try to pull you out?' asked Robin.

'On no account come near me, or you may sink in, and that might be fatal as you are so much shorter than I.'

*He looks the short one!* thought Robin, and he simply couldn't help giggling inside himself, as Mr Wood continued, 'I might have sunk right in if I had not provided myself with a broomstick and pushed it through the sleeves of the scarecrow's coat. The broomstick gave extra support. Luckily it is a stout one. I found it on the site of a gipsy encampment.' (*Lucky he didn't take Gummidge's arms or legs,* thought Robin.) 'I don't *think* I can sink any further as I seem to be standing on a tree root.'

'Have you been there long?' asked Robin.

'Since three o'clock this morning precisely. It was then that the phenomenon occurred.'

Robin wrinkled his forehead, and asked, 'D'you mean you sank in then?'

'Yes, young man. And such a sinking! It was as though thousands of tiny invisible hands were dragging me slowly downwards. I was standing, perfectly still, when my descent began. The earth *may* have a quick-sand quality or there *may* be a hidden bog, but do you know what I suspect?'

Through his dark glasses Mr Wood peered at Robin, who shook his head.

'I suspect the action of moles. I have never seen so many mole-hills. It may be that I have stumbled by chance on one of the great mysteries and miracles of nature. It is tremendously exciting.'

'You aren't going to stay there, are you?' asked Robin.

'Yes, for a little longer at least – possibly until this afternoon. What does a little discomfort matter when one is working in the very lap of Dame Nature herself?'

'I dunno,' said Robin. 'What about food? I could bring you something.'

He was beginning to admire Mr Wood. He might be peculiar, but most people would have made a fuss if they had found themselves nearly up to the chin in earth. They wouldn't have wanted to stay there.

'Could you lend me a handkerchief?' asked Mr Wood.

Robin felt flattered – not many people would have cared to borrow the handkerchief that he pulled from his pocket. Gold paint from the nuggets, bicycle-oil, jam- and toffee-stains made a pattern on cotton that had once been white.

'No, don't throw it. If I stretch my arm out far, I shall disturb the earth even more. Don't come too close to me or you will sink in. Please describe a circle.'

'A circle,' repeated Robin, trying to think of the right words, 'a circle – well, a circle's a sort of piece of round space with a line round it.'

'No, no! You mistake my meaning!' Mr Wood sniffed impatiently and urgently. 'Will you make a detour in order that you may come closer to me IN safety and WITHOUT trampling the earth.'

*A Day Tour?* wondered Robin. *He must be round the bend.*

Between sniffs, Mr Wood explained what he meant. The boy was not to walk straight forward, but was to circle the ground, coming closer and closer until the handkerchief was nearly in reach of the man's hand.

*I could have pushed it to him on a twig,* he thought, as he 'circled' making one broad track.

At last the handkerchief changed hands, and Mr Wood buried his nose in it thankfully.

'Now you must leave me. Silence is absolutely necessary if the moles are to show themselves or if I am to hear them at work.' Mr Wood's nose was pink with cold, and his cheeks were almost pink with pleasure. 'This is a most marvellous opportunity. I have never discovered such a wonderful 'hide'. Just think – if moles *should* appear, I shall be able to observe them almost at eye-level. Just think!'

Robin thought, *You could see them like that if you were lying down, all flat and comfy.*

As though he had guessed the thought, Mr Wood re-marked, 'If I were lying down I should not be so well concealed. Thank you for your kindness, my boy. There is just one more thing – will you be so good as to go to that *Treasure Ship* at four o'clock. If I have not returned, please ask the members of the Fur, Fin and Feather Society to postpone their tea, and come here at once. Ask them to bring their digging tools, and notebooks.'

'O.K.!' said Robin.

'Perhaps you will lead them to this place. Please do not breathe a word to anyone else – promise me that?'

'O.K.!' said Robin again.

He was hungry, and bacon (eggs, too, with any luck) might be sizzling in a frying pan at Finch Cottage.

The morning dragged on rather slowly after that. Robin found that waiting for four o'clock was very nearly as difficult as his attempt to wait for midnight had been. He did not go near *The Treasure Ship* for fear Miss Dollit should ask awkward questions and because he had promised to keep Mr Wood's secret.

All the same he longed to know if Worzel Gummidge had done much damage to the good blue suit and bowler hat, if he had returned to the summer-house and I F (this was the most important) *he* had 'learned the moles to learn Mr Wood not to go badger-badgering'. He wanted to know what would happen next!

In the middle of the morning, while his mother was 'turning out' the sitting-room, Robin dodged up to his bed-room, pulled the clothes-line out of the drawer, and untied the knots. It seemed a very long time since last night – a very long time indeed. He yawned as he arranged the clothes-line into a neat bundle and pushed it back into the drawer. His bed looked very comfortable. He had been awake for much longer than usual the night before, and he had been up much earlier this morning. Could it only be this morning? It felt like a week ago.

*Think I'll finish my book!* yawned Robin.

At half-past twelve, his mother, bringing up some shirts that had been aired above the kitchen stove, found him curled up and sleeping on the bed. Earth from the mole-hills clung to the soles of his shoes, and a scattering lay on the coverlet.

Mrs Finch, as is the way of mothers, put a hand on his forehead to feel if it were hot, and Robin awakened with a start to hear her asking, 'Don't you feel well, dear?'

'Whasser time?' he asked.

'Dinner will be ready in half-an-hour – liver and bacon.'

'Good-oh!' said Robin.

'I suppose that walk before breakfast made you tired, but you *might* have taken your shoes off before lying down.' Mrs Elliot scooped some mole-hill dust into the palm of her hand. 'Did you go for a very long walk?'

'Sorry!' said Robin, apologizing for the earth instead of answering the question.

'Did you go far?'

'Not FAR – just sort of not FAR. I'll go and wash now.'

Robin scrambled off the bed, and hurried into the bathroom.

So the questions had begun! At any moment his mother might ask him if he had seen anyone during his morning walk.

All through dinner he kept his mouth as full as possible so that he could not answer quickly AND politely. There was only one question.

'Are you going to play with Marlene this afternoon?'

'No,' mumbled Robin, 'I'll look after Mary Lou.'

His parents exchanged the sort of glances that meant 'Is it quite natural? Is he quite well? Is he being too good to be true?'

Robin could *feel* the glances, though he stared down at his plate and piled his spoon with jam roly-poly.

'There's nothing wrong with your appetite, anyway!' said his mother.

The afternoon dragged by. Mary Lou was rather difficult and whiney. She didn't want to pick daisies or buttercups or to play horses. She wanted to explore the coalshed: Robin, busy with his own thoughts, left her there while he rushed into the cottage to look at the kitchen clock for the tenth time. Yes, it was half-past three, so if he washed his face and hands slowly and sleeked his hair slowly, and walked very slowly to *The Treasure Ship*, he would not be too early.

Actually he was a little late because he was waylaid by his mother, who had discovered Mary Lou tobogganing down a heap of delightfully slithery skiddy coal-dust.

'Really, Robin, it would have been less bother if I'd looked after the child myself. Now I shall have to wash all her clothes and her hair and everything. How could you have let her get into such a mess?'

Robin shuffled, and hoped that the questions were not going to begin.

'Go up to the bathroom and run a bath of nice warm water. Don't forget to test it with your elbow. I shall want a good deep bath, and I can't have Mary Lou running about and messing up the bath towels while I mix the water. I want to pop her straight in as soon as I've undressed her. I've never seen such a sweep!'

Hot water gushed in an almost boiling stream from the hot tap, but the cold water ran in a determined (or so it seemed to Robin) trickle. He tried swooshing the water about with a sponge. He even tried blowing it! At long last, it turned from very hot to hot, and from hot to warm.

'Ready!' he shouted down the stairs, and his mother, carrying Mary Lou almost at arm's length, came up.

'No, wait at the top,' she told him. 'Don't try to push past us or you'll get your jacket black! Where are you going?'

'Out!' said Robin and, luckily for him, Mary Lou began to bellow, so no more questions could be asked.

Marlene, looking very tidy in a clean cotton frock and cardigan, met him outside *The Treasure Ship*, and she spoke importantly, 'Miss Dollit sent a message saying I could come and help with the tea. Did you have a message, too?'

'I've GOT a message,' replied Robin.

The tea-garden looked quite different because the small tables had been moved, and so had the orange umbrellas.

A long trestle-table stretched nearly from one side of the grass to the other, and the members of the Fur, Fin and Feather Society were in their places. They were rather a strange-looking lot. Robin remembered how some keepers at zoos grow to look like their charges, and he supposed that the curious bird-like expressions of some of the people were the result of bird-watching. One had a face that was rather like the face of a tortoise, and another was weasley. He wondered if the secretary was the man with the long shaggy beard that looked such a perfect place for a small bird's nest. The secretary might be a woman, of course. There was one rather kittenish, youngish person.

Miss Dollit greeted the children.

'There you are, Marlene! What a good child! Run into the kitchen, will you, and see if Mrs Dollit wants any help. Ask her not to fill the tea-pots just yet. I don't think they are quite ready for tea – the people, I mean.' She turned to Robin –

'So you've come, too, have you? I don't know that there's

anything for little boys to do. If you stay, you must sit quite quietly on the grass, and not speak a single word.'

'Which is the secretary?' asked Robin. 'I want to talk to him.'

'But I've told you that you mustn't speak a word or interrupt. This is a grown-up meeting. The secretary is with Mr Wood in the summer-house. He met him in the village or somewhere, so I suppose the poor man must have found something to wear or found his own clothes or —'

Miss Dollit broke off, and glanced towards the summer-house.

'Yes, the secretary is coming out now. He's waving his handkerchief to me. That means they're going to begin with the lecture. I must fly to the kitchen, and keep the tea back ... I hope the scones won't go hard ... You can come and tell me when they're ready for tea.'

She hurried back to the house, and Robin was left alone.

It was all very, very puzzling.

A thin man with drooping walrus moustaches was walking down the path from the summer-house. Behind him, moving stiffly but with great dignity, was Worzel Gummidge.

In Mr Wood's neat blue suit, with the bowler hat on his head, and with his stuffing tucked tidily inside his waistcoat, the scarecrow looked quite human. He was not wearing his bottle-straws. True his boots, muddy and gaping at the toes, looked as though they had belonged to a tramp (as a matter of fact, they HAD) but that did not matter. A bird-watcher could be forgiven for wearing muddy boots.

Earthy, in Miss Dollit's jumper, cardigan, pleated skirt and head-scarf, looked very untidy, but at least the skirt was long enough to hide her bottle-straws, and her twiggy fingers were tucked into the red woollen gloves.

The three curious figures reached the head of the table, and the secretary spoke –

'Ladies and gentlemen! It gives me very great pleasure

to introduce our lecturer. Though Mr Wood is not known
to any of you personally, he is no stranger. We have all
read his books.'

(There was slight clapping.)

'I have only just had the pleasure of meeting Mr Wood
AND Mrs Wood. I should have introduced the lady first.'

(Earthy peeped shyly from behind the secretary's back.)

'Now, ladies and gentlemen, I have a delightful surprise
for you. Mr Wood tells me that his wife knows as much
about natural history as he does. That as I need not remind
you is a very great deal. Mrs Wood has kindly consented to
begin with a few words on – er – COMFORTABLE
ANIMALS. Now, Mr Wood, will you sit down? You
must be tired after your night in the open. Mrs Wood, will
you begin, please?'

With a creak and a give-away rustle, Worzel Gummidge
jerked himself down into a chair.

'The poor fellow seems stiff after bird-watching all night,'
whispered one member to another.

Robin sat down on the grass under the shadow of Saucy
Nancy's outstretched arm. He hoped she would not begin
to sing.

'Beggin' your pardon, and if it's all the same to you,'
began Earthy, 'it's *uncomfortable* animals as needs comfortin'.'

'Of course! Of course!' the secretary looked down at a
piece of paper in his hand. 'I do beg your pardon, how
foolish of me. Mrs Wood will talk about COMFORTING
ANIMALS.'

He sat down beside Worzel Gummidge, who spoke
abruptly, 'Entertaining is as entertaining does. When a
spider entertains a fly it's the fly as entertains the spider.
Stands to reason it is.'

Earthy Mangold seemed to forget her audience, and
addressed her husband –

'I'd sooner be the fly, Worzel. I never could abear to

swaller things as goes all of a flutter. They're very disturbin'
to the stummick. And when it comes to swallerin' Daddy
Long Legses —'

Gummidge interrupted, 'There's no need to come swallerin' Daddy Long Legses.'

'Swallerers casn't be choosers, Worzel, not if they happens
to yawn when other things is flying about.'

There was a pause. Gummidge looked sulky, and Robin
could hear two members of the Fin, Fur and Feather
Society whispering together –

'What an extraordinary lecture!'

'They often begin humorously just to catch the attention.'

The secretary whispered to Earthy Mangold, who looked
puzzled, and turned to face her audience.

'I can tell you what happened to lady friend o' mine as
made a habit o' swallerin' white butterflies.'

There was laughter and clapping, and Earthy continued,
but in a reproving voice –

'Very sad case it were. Her work happened to lay in the
allotment. She were a butterfly scarer, and she couldn't
abear to see the way the caterpillars ate the inside o' the
green cabbages. So she said to hersel', "Seein' as my inside's
not green, caterpillars won't want to eat it!" So she kept
her mouth open, and she didn't shut it again – not till she'd
swallered dozens o' butterflies. The poor thing never thought
to think as the chinks o' her stuffin'd been filled with old
brussels sprouts.'

Worzel Gummidge interrupted –

'She must 'a' been daft. Anyone as weren't daft'd know if
they was stuffed with sprouts.'

'It maybe slipped her memory. Anyways, the butterflies
laid their eggs. Then the caterpillars hatched out and they
wriggled and wriggled and gnawed her sprout stuffin' and
itched her innards cruel. She tried scratchin' but she couldn't
scratch deep enough, so in the end she lost patience.'

Gummidge scowled and said, 'If she'd swallered a bucket o' water, she'd 'a' drowned the caterpillars. Stands to reason.'

'She were too tender-hearted for that; asides buckets o' water is heavy things for ladies to carry about in their innards. She were only a little bit o' a thing. Flighty Buzz her name was. In the end she lost patience, and went and lay down on the railway line. She thought maybe the train'd scratch deep enough. So it did, but she were left with a bend in the middle where her front got stuck to her back arter the wheels'd rolled over it. They hung her on a railin' arter that. Folks needs a lot o' comfortin' when they're hangin' upside down on railin's with caterpillars inside o' them.'

Most of the listeners were gaping, and one whispered, 'It's very sad, but sometimes clever men marry the most peculiar women – not that Mr Wood LOOKS clever!'

The secretary, looking very worried indeed, turned to Earthy –

'That was MOST interesting, Mrs Wood, and now —'

But scarecrows are not quick to take hints, and Earthy was fond of her stories, and did not wish to stop –

'The sad thing is if she'd waited till the caterpillars had turned to chrysalises, she'd have had her peace and quiet nat'ral without her back stuck to her front upside down on railin's. There's another friend I happened to know and SHE —'

'Quite! Quite!' interrupted the secretary. 'I can't tell you how interesting that was.'

Robin hugged his knees, and wondered what would happen next.

The secretary was speaking again. 'Before Mr Wood delivers his lecture, we will follow our usual custom of inviting members of the audience to ask any questions they have prepared on the subject of Natural History. Who will ask the first question?'

The kittenish woman stood up and said, 'I wonder if Mr Wood can solve a problem that has baffled me for years. Why do so many hens begin to moult in cold weather instead of in the summer when they would not feel the loss of their plumage so much?'

Gummidge answered slowly and sulkily.

'Hens moult in cold weather acos hens is daft. No bird as wasn't daft'd sit on chiny eggs in hope o' a fluffy hatch out. All hens is daft.'

Kitten-face giggled.

'Then you think some birds are more clever than others?' she asked.

'Stands to reason I knows some birds is more *daft* nor others. Hens is the daftest. Woodpeckers is least daft: they keeps laughing all summer.'

'Do you think, then, that when a woodpecker laughs it is seeing the funny side of something?'

Worzel Gummidge stared at the questioner.

'When a woodpecker laughs, it's seein' ALL the funny sides o' humans,' he said slowly, 'and that's enough to make any bird laugh.'

The kittenish woman sat down, and the man with the shaggy beard asked hastily, 'In your opinion, Mr Wood, do fish FEEL?'

'Ooh aye! Very slippery fish feels, and all fish feels differ – a jellyfish feels oozy, and a eel feels wriggly, and a stickleback feels stickly!' shouted Gummidge.

'Baby eels is lucky!' remarked Earthy. 'Very lucky baby eels is acos their mothers has got such long laps. Mothers needs to be all sorts o' shapes to be comfortin'. An earwig's got a short skiddy hard little lap, still it's got pincers to catch the babies with. I once happened to know a mother hedgehog and —'

The secretary jumped up, and spoke very quickly –

'I am sure, ladies and gentlemen, that you will all wish

to join me in thanking Mr Wood for answering your questions, and in thanking Mrs Wood, too, for – for – er – what she has said. I feel we should postpone the lecture until after tea.'

A great deal of very loud clapping followed this announcement. Perhaps the members of the Fur, Fin and Feather Society were eager for their tea, and were longing to talk about 'Mr and Mrs Wood'.

The applause seemed to annoy Worzel Gummidge, for the louder it grew the more indignant he looked, and even Earthy had an offended air.

Both scarecrows shambled to their feet.

'Stands to reason we'll not stay to be shooed at!' announced Worzel Gummidge. 'We could shoo back at you, but we'll not demean oursel's.'

Little Earthy spoke boldly, but in a trembling voice. 'Beggin' your pardon, and if it's all the same to you, we could shoo *better* nor you, seein' it's our jobs!'

She brought both her arms forward, and padded the palm of one glove against the other several times.

Gummidge nodded so violently that Mr Wood's bowler tilted forward above one of his eyes.

'We're not goin' acos we're scared and shooed at,' he said, 'we're goin' acos we'll not demean oursel's to stay. Come on, Earthy.'

In the silence that followed, Gummidge, followed by Earthy, left the table. A few inches of polished broomstick showed between the tramp's boots and the edges of Mr Wood's trousers. Miss Dollit's pleated skirt swept the grass behind Earthy.

'How very peculiar!' said the secretary limply. 'I feel I should apologize to you all for inviting Mr Wood to speak. I had heard that he was a most excellent lecturer. He wrote a perfectly normal and most courteous letter in reply to mine.'

The scarecrows did not, as Robin expected, pause by the summer-house, but went, in their offended way, into the orchard.

'I do apologize,' repeated the secretary. 'I realize now that I should have interviewed Mr Wood before asking him to lecture. But, after all, we have all read his books, haven't we?'

Several members of the Fur, Fin and Feather Society agreed how much they had enjoyed Mr Wood's books, and the secretary looked a little comforted.

'Perhaps we should have tea now?' he suggested.

Robin remembered that it was his duty to tell Miss Dollit when tea should be brought into the garden. He would do that, and then he would discover what had happened to the real Mr Wood. It was too late now to give his message to the secretary, and it would make far too much muddle.

He hurried into *The Treasure Ship*.

Robin, as he hurried to the station, wondered why life should be made so difficult for children, and particularly for boys. Grown-up people were not interrupted when they had important things to do.

*Miss Dollit wouldn't have dared ask Captain Conway or Dad to run along to the station, and ask the Rowstock brothers to be sure to bring a crate of china to* The Treasure Ship *as soon as it arrived at Scatterbrook. No! Miss Dollit might have said to Dad, 'If you happen to be passing the station, would you be so very kind as to ask if my china has arrived? If it has, will you tell the Rowstock brothers that I need it urgently.' She wouldn't have said 'Run along, dear, and don't dawdle!'*

These were the words Miss Dollit had used as soon as Robin had told her that the members of the Fur, Fin and Feather Society were ready for tea. AND she had opened the front door so that he had no chance of taking the pleasanter way through the orchard, where he might have had a chance of speaking to Worzel Gummidge and Earthy.

*What do silly old crates matter?* thought Robin, as he dawdled along the main street of Scatterbrook.

He was half-way to the station when he remembered that there might be time for adventure even now. Perhaps Mr Wood was mole-watching still. Perhaps he had sunk deeper and he (Robin) could rescue him at peril of his own life. Then he would be rewarded and anything might happen.

He broke into a run.

The Rowstock brothers were not in the station yard. The great crane was idle, and the coal cart was empty.

Robin decided that he had better go to the Waiting Room, and see if the crate happened to be there, so he hurried out of the yard.

His Aunt Ruby called to him from the back door of Station Cottage where she lived.

'Don't come too near me,' she said, 'I've had a most shocking cold – that's why I haven't been to see your mother lately. How is she?'

Robin said that his mother was very well. Impatiently jigging from one foot to another, he answered questions about his father, about Mary Lou, about the garden at Finch Cottage and about himself.

'I'd like to ask you in,' said his Aunt Ruby, 'but I don't want you to run the risk of catching my cold and passing it on to Mary Lou. That would never do, would it? Did you come on purpose to see me?'

'No,' said Robin, and told his aunt that he was looking for the Rowstock brothers.

'They've been gone a long time. Bert' (he was one of the porter-ticket-collectors) 'hasn't come back from his tea yet. There's no train for half an hour, so he won't be likely to hurry himself. There's nobody on the platform, only a stranger – a man in a bowler hat. I saw him through the front window, not more than a minute ago, and I thought to myself, "You'll have a long wait for the train!" Well, perhaps you'd better see if the crate's in the Waiting Room. Tell Miss Dollit I'll hustle up those Rowstock brothers for her.'

A sneezing attack interrupted his Aunt Ruby's talk, and Robin was able to escape.

Worzel Gummidge, mercifully alone, was in the Waiting Room.

'I'm waitin' for me own clothes,' he explained. 'That badger-badgerer as took 'em told Miss Dollit yesterday he'd be goin' back by train. It'll take me too long to get these clothes the way I likes 'em. Asides, the badger-badgerer went off with my pocket-stuff.'

'What sort of stuff?' asked Robin.

'There was a part-parched worm on a bit o' damp moss as Earthy were comfortin'. She'd not like *that* to go to Lunnon. There was banana-skin hankerchers and all sorts. I don't fancy sharing my hankerchers with strangers.'

Memories of the morning rushed back into Robin's mind. He had lent his own handkerchief to a stranger, and where was that stranger now?

There were so many questions to be asked that he could not think of them in the right order or ask them in the right order, or finish them, even.

'Did you . . . ?' he asked. 'The moles, I mean . . . ? Were there quick-sands or was it moles?'

'Stands to reason it were moles,' answered Gummidge. 'I said I'd learn the moles to learn that badger-botherer not to bother badgers, and they learned him! Earthy went on about it. She said I shouldn't 'a' set *all* the moles to work – not all the old uncles and aunties an' granfers. Earthy said as the old *great* granfers and granmas'd find it heavy work underminin' a badgerer as was so determined. Earthy were wrong same as she mostlings is. Ooh aye! The oldest moles did their learnin' same as I learned 'em. They come from differ bits o' the world, moles did.'

'They couldn't have come over the sea,' argued Robin.

'Moles don't come *over*, they comes *under*!' said Gummidge scornfully. 'Very obedient the moles was – obedient and hard-workin'. Interferin' folks needs a lot o' shiftin' and that badger-badgerer were THAT interferin'! Very intelligent, moles is: they knows a lot more nor humans knows. Moles's hands is allus clean. The dirtier they works the cleaner their hands gets. If humans was to stop washin' they'd give theirsel's and their hands a chance. They never lets the clean settle, and there's more clean nor dirt in the world. Stands to reason – else the place'd be all dustbins and rubbish heaps.'

The idea seemed very reasonable to Robin, but he could not enjoy it properly because he still felt anxious about poor Mr Wood.

'Those moles?' he asked, 'are they – are they —?'

'Moles knows when to stop workin',' replied Gummidge. 'They'd not want that badger-badgerer litterin' up their tunnels year in, year out. Asides, I'd sent Bessie, the one-horned cow, to lend a horn. You knows Bessie?'

Of course Robin knew Bessie: she was his favourite among all Farmer Braithewaite's dairy herd, but he could not think why she should have been asked to lend her one and only horn.

'Ooh aye!' continued Gummidge. 'I were just back from learnin' Bessie when I were told to answer all them daft questions, and talk to all them daft humans. Very impullent they was to start clappin' at me and Earthy. Stands to reason we went away.'

'But,' said Robin, 'when people clap at school concerts and things, they do it because they're pleased.'

'A long way back afore me granfer were set up, farmers used to put human childers in orchards and learn 'em to clap at birds to shoo 'em off of the fruit trees. I knows what clappin' means, stands to reason I does. Clappin's a way o' sayin' *Shoo* to little daft fruit-eatin' birds. I'll not demean mesel' to be shooed at as though I were a daft little fruit-eatin' bird peckin' upside down at a cherry. It's enough to make anyone sulk, and I'll keep on sulkin' till that badger-badgerer brings me own clothes back.'

Gummidge, tilting backwards until Mr Wood's bowler hat rested against a brightly-coloured poster of the Isle of Wight, settled himself into a sulking attitude.

Before he closed his eyes, he murmured, 'I'll not fancy me clothes – not arter that badger-badgerer's been inside of 'em.'

A sulky human is poor company enough, but a sulking scarecrow is very much worse because a scarecrow sulks so thoroughly.

Robin wandered out on to the platform.

It was lucky he did because a curiously sad-looking and dishevelled person was walking towards the Waiting Room. Mr Wood was shaking earth from Gummidge's old trousers, and scooping handfuls of it from the pocket of the coat.

'Coo!' said Robin.

'You may well use that deplorable word, though I prefer to hear it coming from the beaks of doves,' said Mr Wood. 'Did you give my message to the Secretary?'

'Sorry!' said Robin. 'I couldn't because —'

'It is just as well. It would have been useless for the members of the Fur, Fin and Feather Society to have examined the results of all my patient observation. All my time has been wasted. They came trampling all over the place.'

'Who?' asked Robin.

'Cows, my boy, at least a dozen cows. I do not object to bovines when one meets them on the level, so to speak, but when they begin to browse upon one's hat, and explore one's face with their tongues, it is too much of a good thing.'

Mr Wood flung a very earthy primrose root from a pocket, and then pulled out a banana skin.

'How could *that* have got there?' he asked. 'Never mind, as I was saying, the cows trampled the ground all round me until I felt like a plant that has been well heeled into the earth.'

'Coo!' said Robin, who had often helped his father to heel cabbages into the garden at Finch Cottage. It was a satisfying job – one trod all round the plants, and then stamped hard.

'That's not the worst of it,' continued Mr Wood bitterly. 'All the mole-works have been so firmed and trodden down that it will be impossible to examine them. In fact, I was so

wedged that I had the greatest difficulty in extricating myself. If I had not managed to cling to a cow's horn —'

'Coo!' repeated Robin.

'In the circumstances *Moo* might be the better word!'

Mr Wood looked so solemn, and spoke so sadly, that
Robin was not sure if he meant to be funny or not.

'It was a one-horned cow, and singularly inquisitive. I
gripped its horn and tried to push its face away from mine.
The creature moved backwards, and I left the ground as
swiftly as a cork leaves a bottle.'

Now Robin, by putting a finger into his mouth, and pushing it against his cheek, and pursing his lips and pulling the
finger out, could make exactly that same noise. The trick
had taken him weeks of practice, but he had not done it for
a long time, and he did not *mean* to do it then.

Somehow his finger seemed to find its own way to his
mouth, and then there was a most satisfactory pop.

'Like that?' whispered Robin, and waited for Mr Wood
to be angry – not to pat him on the back, and exclaim, 'Just
like that! My boy, I am sure that I could teach you to
imitate the songs of birds and the voices of many woodland
creatures. You have natural ability!'

For the second time within an hour Robin considered
the extraordinary ways of grown-up people, who were so
often cross when they might have been expected to be pleased,
and delighted when they might, quite reasonably, have been
annoyed.

'Yes, yes,' continued Mr Wood, 'you have a natural gift
for imitating noises. If, when you leave school, you would
care to develop the gift, please write to me. I will give you
my card –'

He fumbled in the pocket of Worzel Gummidge's coat,
pulled out another banana skin, sighed, and flung it down.

'Just for the moment I had forgotten my predicament,'
he said. 'What the members of the Fur, Fin and Feather

Society will think of me, I dare not imagine. I could have shaken off the loose mole-worked earth easily enough, and should not have been too conspicuous when walking down the village street. I had planned to change my clothes in the summer-house unless the members of the Fur, Fin and Feather Society had joined me in the wood, but the trampling of the cows seems to have imbedded the earth into the very fabric of these clothes.'

Mr Wood scrubbed hopelessly at Gummidge's earth-encrusted coat.

'I could not have walked along the main village street looking like THIS, could I?'

'No,' agreed Robin, though he was not at all fussy about a little earth or mud.

'So I came by byways to the station. Fortunately the others are returning to London by coach. I shall hope to find a place in an empty carriage. When I reach London I can take a taxi. Will you be so kind as to ask Miss Dollit to post my suit to me. Naturally, I will refund the postage.'

Robin was saved from the difficulty of answering because Mr Wood began to behave in the most extraordinary way. He slapped his pockets, and pulled out more earth and more banana skins. He undid the one button of Gummidge's coat, and fumbled in the places where waistcoat pockets would have been if he had been wearing a waistcoat.

'My ticket!' he exclaimed, 'I left my ticket in my *own* pocket, and my money is there too. I shall *have* to return to *The Treasure Ship* and collect my clothes!'

Robin thought swiftly. Worzel Gummidge was waiting for his clothes, sulking for the need of them, and Mr Wood was in despair.

'It's O.K.!' he said, 'your suit's in the Waiting Room!'

Then he turned and sprinted along the platform, over the crossing, and along the bit of rough ground that led from the other platform to the signal box.

'Coo!' he said, as he propped himself against the iron ladder and looked back at Scatterbrook Station. 'Coo!'

There was nobody on the platform, so Mr Wood must be in the Waiting Room with Worzel Gummidge.

Was Mr Wood capable of undressing a scarecrow? How was Gummidge behaving? Would Mr Wood dress him in his own old clothes? Was the money safe? What about the ticket?

All Robin knew was that he could not have stayed to act as interpreter for a scarecrow and a badger-badgerer.

Mildew Turmut was waving her red flag above the cabbages in the railway allotment, and she was blowing her whistle furiously.

Robin hurried to join her.

Mildew dropped the whistle from her mouth, and spoke excitedly –

'Take my flag, and stop the train when it goes through on its way to Lunnon. It's infringin' the by-laws to throw rubbish out o' trains.'

Mildew waved her green flag over what looked like a heap of old sacks, a clutter of sticks and a tangle of tarred boot-laces.

Robin recognized Hannah Harrow, and the invalid scarecrow, who was lying on her back, gave him a sickly smile.

'I were broadenin' me mind,' she said. 'Upsidaisy told me as travel broadens the mind. Me mind's been sadly narrow ever since a donkey mistook me poor head for something it wanted to eat. Me poor head was half-way down its throat afore it changed its mind, but it were too late then: me mind were sadly narrowed.'

Certainly Hannah Harrow's head looked longer and narrower than it had done in the old days. Sawdust had trickled from her thicker leg, and lay in a little heap beside some seedling lettuces.

'I've been shuntin' up and down in trains this past week,' she moaned. 'I stows away among the stokin' coal, but soon as the stoker finds me he throws me out. It's very disheart'nin' for a lady as wants to broaden her mind by travel to be kep' on bein' throwed out afore her mind has a chance o' swellin' sideways.'

'It's against the by-laws for ladies or rubbish or anything to be throwed out from trains,' persisted Mildew Turmut. 'You looks more rubbish nor lady, Hannah Harrow – very second class you looks – all railway smuts and cheap boot-laces.'

Hannah Harrow clawed at a cabbage stump with her fruithook hand, and dragged herself into a sitting position. Then she tried to arrange the straggles of her boot-lace hair.

'There's other ways o' travel asides trains,' said the Railway Scarecrow reprovingly. 'There's coal carts and aeroplanes – very second class and noisy.'

'I'd get the dizzies if I were throwed out o' aeryoplanes,' objected Hannah Harrow, 'and bein' light-headed and narrow-minded I might stick half-way through the sky. There'd be no company there acos the birds is in such a hurry they'd not spare time to talk about illnesses. Last time I were throwed out o' the train, I fell down by ever such a sufferer, and I told her all about me operation when I was half-swallered by the donkey.'

'Seein' you was only *half* swallered, it were only *half* a operation,' argued Mildew Turmut in such a Gummidgy way that Robin was surprised until he remembered that she was only sister to the chief scarecrow of Scatterbrook.

Hannah looked deeply offended, but continued her story. 'This fellow-sufferer listened more nor she talked acos she suffered with her teeth. She'd been fixed up with a mouse-trap one side of her mouth but the trap weren't wide enough, so they made up with a coupla rows o' pins on tother side. They must 'a' looked pretty all set in pink paper.

Then one day she fancied ant-eggs for her dinner.'

'Ants' eggs?' said Robin, thinking this was a peculiar diet for a scarecrow.

'She were a goldfish scarer, same as I'll be if I ever cures mesel'.'

'But what does a goldfish scarecrow *do*?' asked Robin.

'She stands near a goldfish pond, or sits in a canvas chair, and scares away the fish-eatin' birds. It's a daintier job nor crow-scarin'. This fellow-sufferer were dainty. She were nibblin' ant-eggs ever so dainty with her pin teeth till the mouse-trap went off, and her mouth were pinned together one side. It were pinned firm acos she'd *two* rows o' pin teeth – one top, together bottom. It must have gave her a sad determined look one side, but she's half cured since the pins rusted through. She lost her job arter that because the chronic clickin' o' the mouse-trap kept the goldfish from their sleep. Chronic clickin's very disturbin' to fish that needs their sleep.'

Robin remembered that Miss Dollit had told him she meant to keep goldfish in the 'ornamental pool' in *The Treasure Ship* garden, but before he could say so, he heard the chuff-chugging of the train leaving Scatterbrook Station.

Mildew Turmut, brandishing her red flag, stepped forward, and planted a sardine-tin shoe in Hannah Harrow's lap. The invalid scarecrow's screams were louder even than the shrill blasts from the Railway Scarecrow's whistle, but the train puffed and rumbled on its way. Most of the carriages were empty, but as the last one passed the allotment, Robin caught a glimpse of a passenger. A man in a bowler hat was sitting in a corner seat. Mr Wood was on his way to London.

Soon, only a few wisps of smoke, rising to join the April sky, remained to show that the peace of Scatterbrook Station had been disturbed by a train.

On the distant platform Bert was busy with a broom, and

Robin guessed that Worzel Gummidge had lost his banana-skin handkerchiefs for ever.

Mildew Turmut dropped the whistle from her mouth, and lifted her sardine-tin shoe from Hannah Harrow's lap. Then she peered down at the trickle of sawdust by the lettuce seedlings.

'Slugs dotes on sawdust!' she said. 'Railways that don't employ scarecrows on their allotments mixes slug poison with sawdust, and the slugs eats it hearty. They'll like your stuffin' I wouldn't wonder, Hannah Harrow! You can stay if you likes, and save me the trouble o' slug scarin'.'

'Very infectious, slugs is!' moaned Hannah Harrow, clutching at the cabbage stump with her hooky hand. 'I'll not stay here to catch the slugs. I'll go along with Robin or I'll broaden me mind with coal-cart travel, same as you said, Mildew Turmut!'

But Robin, now that all the excitement of last night and today was over, began to feel very peculiar indeed. His head ached, his legs felt wobbly and wonky. He felt hot, and then he felt cold – as though icicles were trickling down his spine. Then he felt hot again, and very, very thirsty.

Scarecrows didn't matter any more, nor did Mr Wood, nor Worzel Gummidge, nor *The Treasure Ship*, nor Saucy Nancy, even.

Bed was the only thing that mattered – bed and a hot-water bottle or an ice-water bottle. (His face *felt* as red as his red hair.) He wanted to be young again – as young and as little as Mary Lou – to be put to bed by his mother, and to hear her say (because the shivers had begun again), 'I'll bring you a nice hot drink, love. Just you lie still.'

Robin needed his mother very, very badly indeed.

'Got to go home now,' he said.

## 13 Earthy Mangold Pays a Visit

Robin had not caught his Aunt Ruby's cold, but from somewhere or other he had managed to pick up chicken-pox. For days he was hot and very, very bothered. The nights were spent in tossings and turnings and strange dreams. He dreamed he was in a scarecrow hospital and being nursed first by Worzel Gummidge, who argued that the best cure for anything was to stand out in the rain and flap at crows.

Earthy was the kindest of the 'dream-nurses' but she insisted on filling his bed with numbers of little creatures in need of 'comforting'. There were goldfish – in and out of bowls – young hungry starlings, overturned beetles, and worms on little pillows of moss.

Hannah Harrow was the worst of all. In his dreams, she wore a nurse's cap over her boot-lace hair, and wandered saggingly about the ward and moaned about diseases. Since she was a night-nurse, she insisted on sharing Robin's bed because she said that she was a great deal worse than he was.

Saucy Nancy was rough and noisy but bracing. She rolled him 'in the scuppers' which had appeared mysteriously at one end of the ward, put barnacles all over him (these tickled frightfully, but as soon as Robin scratched them off his prickling chest, new ones appeared). While the figure-head was 'sousing him in bilge-water' she sang strange wild lullabies in which scarecrows and sea creatures were strangely mixed up. The words of one were sung to the tune of *Billy Boy*:

'Will you sail along o' me, Earthy dear,
Earthy dear?
Will you sail along o' me,
Me, Earthy dear?
  I will sail along o' thee
  Just so long as he's with me –
  Me Gummidge filled with his rummage,
  Oh, me Worzel who's so queer.

Will you sail along o' me, Worzel Gum,
Worzel Gum?
Will you sail along o' me,
Me Worzel Gum?
  I will sail along o' thee,
  For I wants to see the sea
  And scarin' gets a bit wearin', Oh!
  To sulky Worzel Gum.

Will you sail along o' me, Mildew T,
Mildew T?
Will you sail along o' me,
Me Mildew T?
  I will sail along o' thee,
  And I'll scare the tides at sea.
  The tide'll turn if I'm idle, so
  I'll sail along o' thee.

Will you sail along o' me, Upsidai,
Upsidai?
Will you sail along o' me,
Me Upsidai?
  I will sail along o' thee,
  And I'll eddicate the sea,
  For sea-legs needs to be three legs,
  So I'll sail along o' thee!

Will you sail along o' me, Hannah H,
Hannah H? —'

'Well!' said Robin's mother, and the scarecrow ward
vanished, and Robin was out of the scuppers and back in
his own bed. 'Well, I've heard people talking in their sleep –
your Dad does it sometimes, and Mary Lou whimpers –
but I've never heard anyone sing in his sleep. You must
be better!'

It was several days after the beginning of the chicken-
pox, and Robin was better though he was so prickly and
tickly still that he longed to scratch his skin right off.

Two days later he was very, very much better, and the
morning after that he felt quite well.

'But you won't be able to go into the village yet awhile.
You don't want to give chicken-pox to other children, do
you?'

Robin supposed that he did not.

'And you'll have to keep away from Mary Lou,' continued his mother. 'That will mean spending a lot of time
in your room. I'm afraid it will be dull for you, but you'll
just have to make the best of it.'

*Dull?* thought Robin. *It'll be AWFUL! There's nothing to do
in bedrooms except read and draw and paint and look out of the
window, and then there's nothing to see.*

He wished he could have a scarecrow visitor. Scarecrows couldn't catch chicken-pox – well, Hannah Harrow
might!

'Marlene had chicken-pox last year, so I've asked her to
come and play in the garden this afternoon. I'm taking
Mary Lou to the Institute meeting with me, and your Dad's
going to give Mr Braithewaite a hand in the greenhouse.
It'll be nice to see Marlene again, won't it?'

Robin nodded, but not very eagerly. Marlene would be
better than nobody. Anyway she could tell him if Worzel
Gummidge had returned from the station.

Marlene, when she arrived, was full of most important news about *The Treasure Ship*. Lots of people had been to tea, lots of antiques had been sold AND Miss Dollit's pencils-with-hats, AND Marlene's own gilded shell ash-trays, and Mrs Dollit had sold dozens of scones.

THESE were not the things that Robin wanted to know.

'Where's Worzel Gummidge?' he asked.

'Oh, HIM!' (Marlene was more interested in velvet pin-cushions than in scarecrows), 'he's back in the drain-pipe. You've never seen such a sight as he looks! I've been stick-shells – oyster shells – all round the ornamental pool. I found them in Mrs Conway's dustbin. She must eat a lot of oysters.'

Robin, feeling fractious after chicken-pox, did not mind *what* Mrs Conway ate.

'How's the figurehead?' he asked.

'She's there. The parrot tweaked Mrs Bloomsbury-Barton's best hat off her head, and told her to boil her barnacles! There's lots of birds in the garden now.'

'What sort of birds?' asked Robin.

Marlene told him that Miss Dollit had stocked the 'orna-mental pool' with goldfish, and that a heron had visited the garden and eaten half of them.

'Now she's got another scarecrow from somewhere, and put her in a deck chair by the pool. You never saw such a creature – more like a bunch of sacks and sticks than a scarecrow. Mrs Dollit says it's enough to turn the cream cakes sour.'

Robin guessed that Hannah had become a 'goldfish scare-crow': this was interesting news indeed.

'You'd have thought Miss Dollit would have used the orchard scarecrow,' continued Marlene. 'The lamb doesn't bother about her now that all the new grass has come up. Let's play "houses". I'll be the mother, and you'll be my little boy and do what I tell you. We'll have the coalshed as a house. Come on!'

But Robin did not want to play 'houses'. Nor did he want to do what he was told. 'You said there were lots of birds. I don't call a parrot and an old heron LOTS of birds.'

'It's the seagulls,' said Marlene. 'They come every day – dozens and dozens. They perch on the figurehead and scream, and they perch on the strings Miss Dollit's put up for the fairy-lights. She's going to do suppers as well as teas, and she's going to hang fairy-lights all over the garden, if the silly old gulls don't break the strings. They perch on the gnomes, too, and screech at them. Let's play "houses" now.'

'Oh, ALL RIGHT!'

The game was not a success because Robin was thinking about seagulls and Saucy Nancy and Worzel Gummidge. The sight of the Teddy Bear, now almost clean, and lying on its back by the chopping-block, reminded him of Earthy, and her love for 'Thing-love'.

'If you won't play *properly*, I'm going,' said Marlene.

'All RIGHT!' said Robin.

As soon as Marlene had gone he shook the sawdust from the Teddy Bear. He would take it to his bedroom and tidy it up. His mother would give him some new ribbon for its neck. He could buy a new bell at the Post Office as soon as he was allowed to go out. Then Mary Lou could have it again. In the meantime, even a Teddy Bear would be a little bit of company.

He was carrying the bear out of the woodshed when the boughs of the elder hedge at the back of the rubbish heap began to wave violently. Two of the boughs parted, and Earthy Mangold walked between them.

'Oh, Robin, love!' she said. 'Oh, Thing-love, I've been so lonesome. I've give over bein' a shepherdess acos Lamb-love won't be shepherdessed no more. Mr Gummidge has gone back to bein' a hat-stand, and he says he doesn't know as hat-stands IS husbins and I'd better go back to spinsterin' till he finds out. And Hannah Harrow's turned into a goldfish scarecrow, and there's seagulls all over the place. I've tried scarin' 'em same as Mr Gummidge and me scared 'em off the furrows in Ten Acre Field but they stretches out their necks and screeches back at me. I'm that lonesome!'

All the time that Earthy had been relating her long list of woes, Robin had been turning an idea over and over, to and fro, in his mind.

He was 'lonesome', too, and the big cupboard in his bedroom was empty. Soon it could make a home for Earthy Mangold until he was free to run in and out of his own home. Earthy could tell him stories every evening while his mother was bathing Mary Lou.

He told the plan to Earthy and, at once, the green tears stopped trickling down the little scarecrow's cheeks.

In another few minutes, after a great deal of tugging and scrambling and scratching of paint, Earthy and the Teddy Bear had been dragged upstairs, and were safely stowed away in the big cupboard.

After that, the days and the nights went by more quickly for Robin, though his mother was worried because he did not want to spend more time in the fresh air of the garden, and did not seem to mind whether Marlene visited him or not.

'The boy seems happy enough,' said Mrs Elliot to her husband, 'but it doesn't seem natural he should be happy cooped up hour after hour all by himself in his bedroom.'

'He'll be out of infection tomorrow,' replied Robin's father, 'then he'll be able to racket round the village and play with all his friends. You see, he'll be as gay as a dog with two tails.'

'I'm sure I hope so. If he doesn't pick up I shall have to ask the doctor for a tonic.' Robin's mother folded up her sewing, and his father knocked out his pipe. 'I've heard him talking to himself, and it's not natural for a boy to do that.'

Of course, Robin had not been talking to himself but to

Earthy Mangold. Of course, he was happy because he had learned so much of the strange ways of scarecrows and had listened to so many stories.

That same night, after his parents had gone to bed, Earthy Mangold scrabbled, as usual, on the inside of the cupboard door. It was her signal for story time to begin.

But when Robin had opened the door, the moonlight, streaming through the window on to the little scarecrow's face, showed him that she was unhappy.

'I'm frettin' for Mr Gummidge,' she explained. 'I casn't think what'll happen if he goes on obstinatin' about bein' a hat-stand. I happened to have a lady friend as tried too hard to be furnyture.'

Robin sat down on the bed because he knew a story was coming.

'Her name was Stuffy,' said Earthy. 'She were called Stuffy acos she happened to be stuffed with horsehair. Her arms and legs happened to be made out o' the arms and legs off of an old arm-chair, and she'd a antimacassar shawl.'

'What's that?' interrupted Robin.

'It were a bit o' stuff that were spread over the backs o' chairs for genelmen to rub their hair-oil on. Stuffy'd 'a' been all right if she'd been content to stay scarecrow shape, and stood light on the front legs that had little wheels on 'em. But nothin'd suit her but to bend her joints till she'd made a lap like a arm-chair.

'When she'd made a lap, a paintin' genelman came and sat on it. He sat so heavy he broke her down. Then he picked hissel' up, and walked away.

'I did me best to comfort her, but it's not easy to comfort a friend that's part lap and part antimacassar, and a face all colours o' the rainbow where the genelman's paints had splashed. It were all right in the end in a manner o' speakin'.'

Earthy sighed, and continued –

'When fifth o' November come, Stuffy were turned into a lap for the Guy Fawkes. It come on to rain, so they never lit the bonfire. There she sits with the Guy on her lap, but seein' his ears is set back'ard, he casn't hear what she says, and seein' his mouth's stiff he casn't speak to her. It's not what I'd call a happy marriage – not all that happy.'

'No,' agreed Robin.

'So I did ought to go back to Mr Gummidge afore he turns to furnyture. Help me out o' the winder, Robin, love, and let me go back to Mr Gummidge. If you throws me out I'll manage somehows!'

But Robin had a better idea. The clothes-line was in the drawer, and Earthy was not at all heavy.

Quarter of an hour later, the moon shone down on a small figure hurrying as quickly as the long pleated skirt would allow towards the elder hedge. The moon shone, too, on the tangled rope that Robin was hauling up through his bedroom window.

# 14 Gulls and Goldfish

The 'day after tomorrow' had turned into 'today'. It was seven o'clock on a dewy morning, and Robin was alone in the garden of *The Treasure Ship*. Well, no, he was not ALONE, but there were no humans in sight.

Saucy Nancy's outstretched arm was making a perch for seagulls. The same birds crowded the strings that held the swinging 'fairy-lights.'

Worzel Gummidge, wearing his earth-stiffened coat and trousers, his battered hat on the back of his head, was planted in his drain-pipe. He looked nearly but not quite the same as usual. This was because he was not in his crow-scaring or 'hat-stand' attitude: his ragged coat sleeves were not flapping in the breeze, and his arms hung down.

Earthy Mangold, smiling happily, stood beside her husband.

Hannah Harrow, slumped into a deck chair, sat beside the 'ornamental pool'.

Saucy Nancy broke into a rusty, creaky song:

> 'Sing me a song of a lass that has gone,
>     Splintered and warped and dry,
> Timbers a-creak, dust on her cheek
>     Now that her tears are dry.
>
> Lend me a hand! Take me from land
>     Down to the sea again,
> There can I guide ships, in their pride,
>     Over the sea to Spain.'

Robin ran under the figurehead's arm, and looked up at her while the seagulls rose in a sleekness of grey and white feathers. One bird kept to its perch on the pointing finger, stretched its long neck, opened its yellow beak with the blaze of orange below, and screeched at the boy.

'It's asking for fish!' said Nancy.

Robin considered. Before he had left Finch Cottage early that morning he had explored his mother's larder.

'There's some finnan haddock at home,' he said.

'Finny haddy! Finny haddy!' creaked Saucy Nancy. 'Finny haddy's got the smell o' land and wood-smoke. A mackerel'd a put the bird in mind o' the sea. Mackerels glint blue and green and silver same as water.'

'Sorry!' said Robin, and he felt sorry, too.

The disappointed seagull flew up into the blue of the sky.

'I'm more parched nor a ship in dry dock,' said Nancy. 'My sort dies on land. Have you watched a ship dyin', shaver?'

Robin, of course, had NOT.

'Many's the time I've seen 'em dyin' on salt mud-flats above high water, with their timbers gapin' and their paint a-peelin' off, and their keels aching for water. Not proper ships – mostly barges – but ships in a manner o' speaking.'

The morning was not being so cheerful as Robin had hoped and expected. 'I could catch a goldfish,' he said, 'I think I could.'

'Goldfish!' repeated Saucy Nancy, 'goldfish! All gloopy and gluppy and blowing bubbles! I sailed with a skipper that kept a goldfish in a bowl in his cabin. The fish glupped till he mixed it up with the compass – THAT bein' in glass, too. The skipper went by the goldfish tail instead o' the compass arrow and we was wrecked off Cape Horn. That WERE a wreck!'

Perhaps because Robin had been standing so still while he was listening to Saucy Nancy's memories, the seagulls returned in their flying masses. One perched on Saucy

Nancy's head, others ranged themselves along her out-stretched arm.

Robin did not notice where the rest perched because Saucy Nancy was singing again:

'Seagulls, seagulls, fly me away to sea,
    To the wind-lashed foam,
    And the gales of home,
And the songs they sing to me –
    To the whales' deep bath
    And the sea-grained path
That leads where a lass would be.

Seagulls, seagulls, quicken your wings and fly
    To the sweeping bays
    Where a lass can laze
And hark to the sirens' cry –
    To the blue and grey
    Of the far-away
Where the sea-line meets the sky.'

Robin left Saucy Nancy, and joined Hannah Harrow by the 'ornamental pool'.

The invalid scarecrow peered at him through the tangle of her boot-lace hair.

'I've scared a heron,' she said. 'I weren't employed to scare seagulls. You don't know what diseases you mightn't get from gulls. I've had most land-illness, I don't want sea-sickness on top of all the other sufferin's.'

Robin left Hannah Harrow, and joined Worzel Gummidge and Earthy Mangold.

'It's all right, love,' said Earthy Mangold, 'Mr Gummidge's give over bein' a hat-stand since I told him I'd as soon be married to a hedgehog as to a bit of furnyture.'

'Ooh aye! Stands to reason,' agreed Worzel Gummidge

cordially, 'hedgehog husbins curls up into prickly balls with their noses pressed into their stummicks.'

'It makes 'em poor company, poor little things,' said Earthy.

'Hedgehog wives does the same. Hedgehog wives' noses presses *harder* into their stummicks.'

'It don't make for happy marriages,' said Earthy. 'A hedgehog wife might be uncurled while her husbin were curled, and then they'd both be lonesome. Worzel and me'll be going back to Ten Acre Field afore long.'

'Ooh aye! Rooks needs scarin' – rooks an' —'

Worzel Gummidge raised a broomstick arm and waved it at a seagull skimming on its way to perch on Saucy Nancy.

'Rooks and pesky seagulls!'

'Saucy Nancy seems to like seagulls,' said Robin.

Slowly and deliberately Earthy turned her back towards the figurehead, and Gummidge spoke sulkily, 'There's some as likes spadgers!'

Robin glanced towards Hannah Harrow. She sat facing the figurehead, but her face, nearly hidden by the tangle of boot-lace hair, was turned sideways.

Robin remembered that the scarecrows had taken no notice of Saucy Nancy during any of his visits to *The Treasure Ship*, nor had she spoken to them.

*Don't scarecrows like figureheads?* he wondered, as he went home to breakfast, *don't they mix? Different sorts of birds don't mix. Starlings don't rest in rookeries. Rooks don't flock with starlings. P'r'aps figureheads like to keep themselves to themselves – like Mrs Kibbins says she does. P'r'aps scarecrows don't like strangers.*

For breakfast there was finnan haddock with poached eggs on top of it: Robin ate a lot, and his father looked across at his mother as though to say, 'The boy's all right again now. What did I tell you?'

The boy felt very much all right as he hurried back to *The Treasure Ship*. Mrs Dollit and Miss Dollit were in the garden, so were the seagulls – more and more and more of them. They circled Saucy Nancy in a white cloud. One, perched on the top of a chimney, was stretching out its neck and screaming loudly as though trying to call all the seagulls from all the seas to visit Saucy Nancy.

'I don't know what to do about them,' said poor Miss Dollit. 'I've been a bird-lover all my life – a *little-bird*-lover – but these are so big and so noisy.'

'Well,' – Mrs Dollit ducked down to avoid a low-swooping gull – 'you asked for them, Phoebe, and now you've got them.'

'Mother, *dear*! I didn't ask for them.'

'If you will put figureheads into tea-gardens, you must expect what figureheads bring along with them. Soon there'll be sharks and whales and shrimps. I wonder you don't use rafts instead of tea-tables!'

Just for a moment Miss Dollit looked as though she thought that would be quite a good idea, but a string holding a line of fairy-lights broke beneath the weight of birds, and her answer could not be heard above their loud indignant voices.

'You'll have to get rid of that figurehead,' said Mrs Dollit, 'it's a perfect magnet for seagulls.'

'I'm rather afraid you may be right, Mother, but I can't understand it. After all, seagulls do fly inland in stormy weather.' (Mrs Dollit stared up at the calm blue sky.) 'Besides we've had the figurehead for some time, and we haven't been plagued by gulls before.'

'They seem to have learned their way now,' said Mrs Dollit grimly.

A particularly bold gull swooped down to the 'ornamental pool' and very nearly caught a goldfish.

Hannah Harrow gave a feeble cry, shook her boot-lace locks and shivered.

'No! No! No! Naughty bird!' cried Miss Dollit, clapping

her hands and dancing round the edge of the water.

The seagull made a laughing noise, and flew to a tree.

'Yes, Mother, I'm afraid you may be right,' repeated Miss Dollit, 'the jolly old figurehead must go. I know what I'll do, I'll find Farmer Braithewaite and ask if he can use her as a scarecrow.'

*No, no*, thought Robin, *not Saucy Nancy! She hates the land*.

While Mrs Dollit argued that the figurehead had not proved herself very useful as a bird *scarer* and Miss Dollit argued that seagulls were good for the land because they ate slugs and insects, Robin listened miserably.

Miss Dollit turned round and noticed him for the first time that morning.

'You could run along to Farmer Braithewaite, couldn't you, dear? No, perhaps you had better help my mother to keep the gulls away from the goldfish. They don't seem to mind poor old lady scarecrow, though the heron was terrified of her. I shan't be long. Keep running round and round the pond, Robin, but don't fall in.'

'If you keep running round and round you'll get dizzy, and then you will fall in,' said Mrs Dollit sensibly, as soon as her daughter had hurried out of the garden. 'You keep away from the pool. I'll look after the goldfish.'

Robin ran across the grass, and spoke to Saucy Nancy.

'Send the gulls away,' he begged. 'If you don't send them away you'll be put into a field, and used as a scarecrow. Do send them away!'

'Blister my barnacles! Boil me in bilge-water!' shouted Saucy Nancy. 'I've been calling the gulls all night, pleading and calling for them to carry me back to sea. I'd not be a gull-scarer, not for all the Spanish gold in Davy Jones's old locker. They ought to rest their wings, though. It's a long flight back, and I'll not be easy carried.'

Tilting her head back, she hummed as the wind hums in rigging. At the sound the circling seagulls settled again, some on her, some on branches and some on the steep roof of *The Treasure Ship*. Mrs Dollit was able to rest her arms, and Hannah Harrow sagged back into the deck chair.

A man pushing a hand-cart walked into the garden, and as he walked he sang in a high whining voice:

> 'Any old rags and bones,
> Any old gramophones,
> Or keys without locks,
> Any old shoes or socks,
> Or broken-down clocks,
> ANY OLD RAGS AND BONES?'

Robin recognized him as Mr Flint, the rag-and-bone man, who pushed his hand-cart from Scatterbrook to Penfold, from Penfold to Dimden and back again to Scatterbrook twice a week when the weather was fine enough. In between times he sorted all the junk he had collected. People said he made a good living, though he looked as shabby as Worzel Gummidge himself.

Mr Flint lived in an old barn surrounded by a stretch of waste land that had been a farmyard once upon a time before the farm was burned down.

> 'Any old rabbit skins?
> Any old jars or tins?'

chanted Mr Flint;

> 'Any old bits or bats,
> Any old slates or slats,
> Any old Sunday hats,
> ANY OLD RABBIT SKINS?'

He set down his hand-cart and shouted, ''Mornin', Mrs Dollit! I've come for the junk you told me to fetch. Lumme! Goin' in for bird-fancyin' are you? Wish those gulls'd come to my yard. I bought a lot of old herring barrels in Dimden, and they need cleaning out. I'll say they do.'

Mrs Dollit left the pool, and came towards Mr Flint.

'The rubbish is in the summer-house,' she said. 'You've been there before, haven't you?'

Mr Flint did not answer. He was staring at Saucy Nancy as though he loved her.

'You'll find all the stuff in the summer-house,' repeated Mrs Dollit.

Mr Flint nodded impatiently and then asked, 'Is the figurehead for sale? Give you a quid for her if she is.'

He pulled a crumpled pound note out of his pocket.

Robin turned away because he didn't want to SEE Saucy Nancy being sold. She was too alive and too lovely to spend her years in Mr Flint's yard among the herring barrels (though she might like those) and the rusty netting and the warped golf clubs and all the land clutter.

He heard Mrs Dollit answering, 'Yes, I can sell the figurehead for a pound. My daughter is out at present, but I feel sure she would agree. The other things are in the summer-house. I'm sure Robin will help you to pack the cart. I must go back to the house now.'

It had happened! Saucy Nancy was sold! Robin felt in his own pockets. If only, he thought, if only he could buy her himself, and set her free, and run away to sea with her. He fumbled desperately but though his four half-crowns made him feel rich, he knew he was not rich enough to bargain with Mr Flint, who was known as SKIN-Flint in the village.

He did not dare to look at Saucy Nancy, but suddenly he heard her voice, singing new words to the rag-and-bone man's tune:

> 'Any good home for me,
> Any good ships for sea,

> Any old spars and sails,
> Any waves with backs like whales,
> Any brave sound of gales,
> ANY GOOD HOME FOR ME?'

'Cor!' exclaimed Mr Flint, 'I thought I'd invented that tune! It shows there's nothing new in the world, doesn't it?'

> 'Any good home for me –
> Any fine ships for sea,
> Any great whale-backed waves
> And salty songs from caves,
> Any home that suits the braves,
> ANY GOOD HOME FOR ME?'

Mr Flint had walked across the grass, and was staring up at Saucy Nancy.

'Cor, what a beauty!' he said, as the seagulls swung and swooped above him. 'So the wooden lady sings, does she?'

Robin didn't bother to answer such a stupid question. Of course Saucy Nancy sang: Mr Flint had heard her.

'Have you got the key?'

'The summer-house isn't locked,' said Robin. 'There isn't a lock.'

'Cor! I'm not so interested in the summer-house now. I want the key to the lady. There's some sort of musical box or mechanical goings-on inside. Must be. They're not run down or out of order either.'

So *that* was what Mr Flint thought of Saucy Nancy – he thought she was a big mechanical toy with no more life in her than the clockwork mouse that had so delighted Mary Lou until its key was lost.

'It must have been wound up quite lately or the works would have rusted, seeing it's been standing out in all weathers. This netting's soaking wet.'

Mr Flint was probing and prodding under Nancy's fishing-net shawl as he tried to find her 'works'.

'Do you think Mrs Dollit keeps the key indoors?'

'No!' said Robin, speaking furiously because he felt that Saucy Nancy was being insulted. Yet how could he give her secret away to this rag-and-bone man, who was going to take her away to his dirty old junk yard?

The seagulls were strangely silent. The parrot peered down from its cage in the apple-tree as Mr Flint dodged round Saucy Nancy, and began to prod her back.

'It's queer,' he muttered, 'salt's working out of her as though she's only just been fished out of the sea. I can't find any works though. Never mind – I'll have a proper look-see when I get it back home.'

Crusty salt tears glistened on Saucy Nancy's cheeks. Her face looked noble but sad.

'She's worth ten quid to me, key or no key,' muttered Mr Flint.

'Quid o' baccy or quid o' cash?' rapped out Saucy Nancy.

Robin saw her lips move but Mr Flint started back. Then he noticed the parrot.

'The old bird didn't half give me a turn,' he said, 'it sounded as though the figurehead was speaking! Now then, sonny, just you nip into the house and ask Mrs Dollit for the key. She's bound to have it. Not that it matters all that much – I daresay I've something at home that'll fit.'

Saucy Nancy shivered so violently that the dew flew from her shawl in brilliant drops.

The rag-and-bone man did not notice because he was walking towards the hand-cart. Over his shoulder he spoke to Robin again –

'I'll be loading the summer-house junk while you're finding the key. Then you can give me a hand with the figurehead and I'll give you a tanner.'

Slowly, very slowly and sadly, Robin made his way over the grass, and as he went he thought – *Sixpence for helping Saucy Nancy to be miserable in a smelly old junk yard! I wouldn't do it for ANYTHING. If only the seagulls would fly away first. P'r'aps she can make them. I'll stay in* The Treasure Ship *for a long time to give them a chance. Coo! I'd like to see Saucy Nancy flying over Mr Flint's head. I'd like to see his face!*

From the sound of eggs being beaten, Robin guessed that Mrs Dollit was making cakes. He didn't interrupt her, but hurried past the kitchen door, and went straight into the shop part of the house.

Sunshine was making the bowl of nuggets in the window gleam like real gold.

*If only they were real,* thought Robin, *if only they were real, I could buy Saucy Nancy. I wonder if Mr Flint would know paint from real gold. But if he didn't it would be sort of stealing, and Dad wouldn't like it.*

He went to the other window and looked across the garden – beyond the silly gnomes, beyond Hannah Harrow in her deck chair, beyond the concrete lamb that had so excited the 'Cruelty Lady' to where the seagulls were clustering round Saucy Nancy. But they were settling on her again – not flying her away. A row of them perched on her arm, wings folded, huddling together as closely as swallows on a telegraph wire. They should, if they were going to fly her away, be under her arm, their wings outstretched, and straining for lifting. The sea-magic was not happening: all the gulls in the garden were very still.

Robin opened the window because he wondered if Saucy Nancy was singing a sea-dirge.

There was no sound except the chinking of glass on glass as Mr Flint tumbled jam-jars into the hand-cart.

Worzel Gummidge was sulking in his drain-pipe, and Earthy stood beside him while bundles of sacks and Miss Dollit's old clothes were piled on top of the jars.

*Now for it!* thought Robin, and ran into the garden, ready to fight for Saucy Nancy because the rag-and-bone man was wheeling the cart towards her.

'Taken your time, haven't you?' snapped Mr Flint. 'Didn't the old lady find the key?'

'No,' said Robin, truthfully enough, but glad he had not been asked if Mrs Dollit had looked.

'It doesn't matter. Now, if you'll catch hold of the netting – keep it free from the stand – I'll look after the figurehead.'

Robin stood firmly, hands behind his back, between Mr Flint and Saucy Nancy. 'What's going to happen to her?' he asked.

'I'll sell it easy enough, else I shouldn't have bought it. I'll sell it to a bloke of the name of Perkins —'

'Mr Perkins?' yelled Robin, and then he felt cold inside as he remembered that Perkins was not an unusual name.

'That's right. He lives on the caravan site, but he's leaving. He made a packet out of the football pools ... Mind yourself, sonny, I don't want to stay here all day.'

Robin skipped aside (it was remarkable how lightly he could skip after hearing the great news) and Mr Flint went on talking as he disentangled Saucy Nancy's fishing-net skirt.

'This Perkins chap thought of buying a pub in Portsmouth, but he's changed his mind. Some don't know when they're lucky! He's buying a boat instead. Give me the land any day! Still I needn't grumble, he said he'd give me a fair price for any ship clutter I could pick up. He's free with his money, I'll say that for him.'

*Free with his money!* Robin chinked his four half-crowns together.

'He's more money than sense if you ask me!' Mr Flint draped the fishing-net over the top of the sundial, and glanced up at the parrot.

'Do you think that old Polly would go for a song?'

*Anything, anyone would go anywhere for one of Saucy Nancy's songs,* thought Robin.

'Do you think Miss Dollit would sell it, I mean?'

'Dunno!' said Robin, 'I can ask.'

Suddenly Mr Flint seemed to have turned into a quite nice sort of man. The world was nice, the morning was lovely, and Saucy Nancy was splendid.

'That's the lad!' said Mr Flint, and Saucy Nancy's lips stiffened into a smile as she was lifted down on to the hand-cart.

Robin followed into the road to see her off.

The gulls went with her, shaking the dust of Scatter-brook from their wings. They screamed above the Post Office. Their shadows startled the dust-bathing sparrow.

Mr Flint sang his old song as the wheels of the hand-cart squeaked beneath the weight of jam-jars, rags, Miss Dollit's old clothes AND Saucy Nancy:

> 'Any old rags and bones,
> Any old gramophones,
> Any old bolts or bars,
> Any old tins or jars,
> Any old junk from cars,
> ANY OLD RAGS AND BONES?'

The figurehead took up the song:

> 'Any new home for me –
> Any salt breath from sea,
> Any salt spray from foam,
> Any more seas to roam,
> Any home? Any home?
> ANY OLD NEW HOME FOR ME?'

Her voice faded away as Mrs Kibbins's cat sprang to the safety of the garden wall, arched her back, and hissed at the seagulls.

Robin felt happy as he ran back into *The Treasure Ship* garden and along the path to the summer-house. He was happy and lonely at the same time.

Earthy Mangold, who had shed her red woollen gloves, patted his arm with twiggy fingers.

'I've been so afeared,' she said, 'I were so afeared that man'd want to take my Worzel. Very upsettin' it'd be to see your husbin took away with a lot o' old rags an' jars. Very insultin' it'd 'a' been.'

'Ooh aye! Stands to reason!' agreed Worzel Gummidge, breaking his sulk for a moment, but settling comfortably back into it again.

'What happened were more insultin'. It's more insultin' when a man as wants old jars an' rags an' all sorts casn't be perlite enough to want Mr Gummidge.'

The Chief Scarecrow of Scatterbrook opened his eyes, and muttered, 'Stands to reason I'll not demean mesel' to be insulted by folks as don't know perlite from impullent. Me and Earthy's goin' back to Ten Acre to go on with our own jobs. I've give over bein' a hat-stand and she's give over bein' a shepherdess. Ooh aye!'

'Oh, Worzel, LOVE!' said Earthy, 'I dotes on Ten Acre, it's so uncomplicate.'

*So everything's all right*, thought Robin. *Saucy Nancy will go to sea, and the Gummidges will go back to Ten Acre, and Upsidaisy will be at school when I go back. EVERYTHING'S FINE.*

On the following pages you will find details of other exciting books from Sparrow.

## THE MIDNIGHT KITTENS

### Dodie Smith

Pam and Tom, orphaned twins, live happily with their grandmother in the country and go to a boarding school. At home for the spring half-term holiday, they become involved in some strange and mysterious happenings. Enchanting wild kittens appear in the orchard, always on the stroke of midnight, and the twins believe that they are magic. They visit a long-deserted, haunted house and meet a lady almost a hundred years old who lived there as a child. She tells them of a secret room and a hidden painting, and, armed with her instructions, the twins return to the house at sunset – and become involved in an adventure which threatens their whole existence.

From the bestselling author of *The 101 Dalmations* and *The Starlight Barking*, books which have become classics of children's literature, this splendid story has a warmth and charm endearing it to grown-ups and children alike.

80p

# A GHOST HUNTER'S HANDBOOK

## Peter Underwood

Long-time ghost expert and hunter, Peter Underwood, tells children all they need to know about ghosts, their habits and habitats. Peter Underwood, who is president of the Ghost Club and copyright holder of the only known photograph of a ghost, has written several books on ghosts for adults, but this is his first book on the subject for children. Serious in approach, it covers everything from how to find a ghost to information on ghosts that have been found in all parts of the world, and includes a section on famous ghosts and haunted houses that can be visited.

85p

# THERESE BIRCH'S
# JELLYBONE GRAFFITI BOOK

For the first time – a collection of the best in graffiti compiled
by children for children.

*Count Dracula drinks Bloody Marys*

*Preserve wildlife – pickle a duck*

*Work fascinates me – I can sit and look at it for hours*

*Humpty Dumpty was pushed*

# The Sparrow Bookshop

Sparrow has a whole nestful of exciting books that are available in bookshops or that you can order by post through the Sparrow Bookshop. Just complete the form below and enclose the money due and the books will be sent to you at home.

| | | |
|---|---|---|
| THE JELLYBONE GRAFFITI BOOK | Therese Birch | 85p |
| THE BOY WHO WANTED A DOG | Enid Blyton | 65p |
| THE BIRTHDAY KITTEN | Enid Blyton | 65p |
| WORZEL GUMMIDGE AND THE TREASURE SHIP | Barbara E. Todd | 85p |
| THE MIDNIGHT KITTENS | Dodie Smith | 80p |
| A GHOST HUNTER'S HANDBOOK | Peter Underwood | 85p |

*Picture books*

| | | |
|---|---|---|
| IF MICE COULD FLY | John Cameron | £1·25 |
| CRAZY CHARLIE | Ruth Brown | £1·25 |
| K9 AND THE ZETA RESCUE | David Martin | 65p |
| K9 AND THE BEASTS OF VEGA | David Martin | 65p |
| K9 AND THE TIME TRAP | David Martin | 65p |
| K9 AND THE MISSING PLANET | David Martin | 65p |

*Total plus postage*

And if you would like to hear more about our forthcoming books write to the address below for the Sparrow News.

**SPARROW BOOKS, BOOKSERVICE BY POST, PO BOX 29, DOUGLAS, ISLE OF MAN, BRITISH ISLES**

Please enclose a cheque or postal order made out to Arrow Books Limited for the amount due including 8p per book for postage and packing for orders within the UK and 10p for overseas orders.

Please print clearly

NAME _____

ADDRESS _____

_____

Whilst every effort is made to keep prices down and keep popular books in print, Arrow Books cannot guarantee that prices will be the same as those advertised here or that the books will be available.